Stalin in the Bronx
and Other Stories

Stalin in the Bronx

AND OTHER STORIES

by Suzanne Ruta

GROVE PRESS : New York

Published by Grove Press, Inc.
920 Broadway
New York, N.Y. 10010

Hortensia and *A Fateful Visit* (here retitled *Stalin in the Bronx*) appeared previously in *Grand Street,* and *The Autograph* in *Ascent.*

These stories are works of fiction. Names, characters, places, and incidents are either the product of the author's imagination or are used fictitiously. Any resemblance to actual events or locales or persons, living or dead, is entirely coincidental.

Library of Congress Cataloging-in-Publication Data

Ruta, Suzanne.
    Stalin in the Bronx, and other stories.

    I. Title.
PS3568.U8135S7   1987   813′.54   87-8507
ISBN 0-8021-0018-X

Manufactured in the United States of America
Designed by Irving Perkins Associates
First Edition 1987

10 9 8 7 6 5 4 3 2 1

Contents

Stalin in the Bronx 1

The Shoe Clerk 16

The Bus 41

The Autograph 63

Soldier's Rest 78

In Fiona's Country 88

Carmela 99

Hortensia 108

At the Border 115

The Actor 133

An Imaginary Line 146

Stalin in the Bronx

It is not generally known that Joseph Stalin visited the United States in the fall of 1936. Although nearly fifty years have gone by, the story has yet to be told. When and if the truth becomes known, many mysteries that have plagued our generation and our parents' before us will be resolved. The tangled skein of relations, between Alger Hiss and Whittaker Chambers will be unraveled to everyone's satisfaction. People who stopped speaking to one another decades ago will be friends again, and those who for years have addressed one another only in print, in public and in the form of invective, will have to find a whole new set of enemies. Some of the people in question are unfortunately well on in years by now, and one can only hope the facts emerge in time for peace to be restored all around.

I stumbled on the truth, or a tiny corner of it at any rate, quite by chance last fall on Cape Cod. My widowed mother was with us for a week in late September, enjoying what she told us, accurately, I'm afraid, was the first real vacation of her life. At low tide on Corn Hill beach she gathered pebbles and shells as earnestly as any of her grandchildren, except that where they were careless and left their treasures for the tide to repossess, she hoarded hers in her purse. Each evening at dinner my husband poured her a first glass of wine and watched it carefully and refilled it as soon as it was half empty, and I thought, seeing how lively and talkative she grew after three glasses, what a pity it was my father never touched a drop.

The day before she was to leave, I invited a neighbor to tea, a woman writer of about my mother's age, whose last book traced the determining role of the KGB in the Berkeley Free Speech Movement, the Columbia sit-ins, the Paris May rebellion and the Prague Spring. This friend and I had agreed, for the sake of friendship, to disagree about politics. She called me a starry-eyed idealist and accused my husband, a disabled veteran, of hating his country. But she also showed us gardens abandoned at summer's end by liberal think-tank professors who had returned to their overpaid (she said) jobs at Harvard and MIT. Together we gleaned the last of the year's tomatoes, parsley and marigolds. Watching her stoop over the unwatered beds, I could see why to her it might appear that the Left ran the country, and I was glad I didn't live on the Cape year round, and thus knew better.

As if to seal a week of the charmed life, my mother and our neighbor hit it off tremendously well. Georgiana was in the backyard inspecting a wild baby rabbit she had found under a hedge and given to our children to raise, but my mother still felt the need to whisper. "I like that kind of woman. Such a nice-looking woman." The writer could have passed for her sister. The two had the same sharp nose and full bosom. My mother's eyes, however, are dark and dreamy while Georgiana's are blue and outward-gazing. She was born in a former British colony and her accent endeared her further to my mother, a staunch Anglophile although she has never left the States. Thanks to the BBC, she says, she doesn't need to.

When, the day before, I showed my mother Georgiana's book, she asked, "Who reads a book that size? It must be one of those they publish with help from the CIA." But now she was delighted to talk about my father with someone she knew would listen sympathetically. There was so much about him she had had to hide from people, different things from different people at different times over the forty years they were together.

I saw at once that the writer's vital period, the time of her life when she had been having the time of her life, coincided exactly with my mother's. It was that privileged period my parents always referred to, with such nostalgia I had to envy them, as "the old days." By which they meant the decade that began with the stock-market crash and ended with the Stalin-Hitler pact.

"Did you know R?" Georgiana named a German refugee who had reached New York in 1938 with tales of Stalinist sabotage of the German anti-fascist left. Not only did my mother know him, she had boarded him for a whole month in the cabin up in Croton-on-Hudson. He was in hiding, or maybe just broke, she couldn't remember which. They were all desperately poor in the old days. Georgiana was terribly impressed. She had heard of R, to her he was a sort of folk hero, but she had never met him. I was glad I could reciprocate for her tips about abandoned gardens by letting her glean now in my mother's memory. And I thought my mother was having a fine time too, but after the writer had left, she worried.

"She must think I was awfully stupid not to remember anything of what R had to tell us. But I was always in the kitchen making dinner. It was such a tiny kitchen. Everyone said"—here she brightened again—"it was a miracle what I could do in that kitchen. The oven floor tilted like this." She cocked her head to one side and giggled, although we had drunk only tea.

"What would your friend have said if I'd told her about the dinner I served Joe Stalin?"

"Joe Stalin, *the* Joe Stalin? When? Where?" I asked. Until this week, her first real vacation, I had always thought of my mother as a tomb, an abyss. She applied the maxim "De mortuis . . ." to the living as well. Living and dead were extended the same courtesy in her speech as a rule. This had a deadening effect on almost every conversation I tried to engage her in, and it is wrong to treat the living as though they too are beyond help or change. But my mother was a fatalist, and had her reasons to be one. The only expressions that came unguarded from her lips were offers of help to friends or even strangers in need. And if the offer was spurned or not properly acknowledged, she might give voice to her resentment. As a source of information about "the old days" she was generally useless. I once tried, for example, to find out from her just when and under what circumstances my father left the party. All I could get from her that day was a story about the well-to-do wife of a *Worker* editor, who phoned one day and said, "Esther, would you like a new winter coat?"

Of course my mother said yes and wondered which it would be, the fur-collared, or the gray tweed, or maybe even the bottle green velvet cape the editor's wife had worn last time she and her husband came for dinner.

"Well, if you want a coat, don't miss the sale in Klein's, on the fourth floor. It's on all week," the woman told my mother, who had not forgiven her, forty years later, for raising and then dashing her hopes.

But now she answered my question about Stalin: "When do you think it was? On that trip to New York he made in thirty-six, to raise money for the Spanish Republic. I missed the big rally at the Garden, but so did Stalin. That in itself is a story I can't tell you today. He never made it out of the Bronx."

"Why not?" I should have stopped her there and then. "Why can't you tell me?" But I knew how skittish her memory was and I hesitated to interrupt. And I was used to letting her make the rules.

"Before he left town, your father's friend Nat brought him up to the Croton place and I made a lemon meringue pie. How I managed in that oven I still don't know. And it was so hot and damp, try making pie crust in that weather."

That bit of information from her bag of old grudges. She had slaved to produce a bit of perfection in an imperfect world and Stalin, I could well imagine, had failed to compliment her on the effort, although he had probably taken a second and perhaps even a third helping. She would have been keeping track.

"I thought Dad already hated Stalin's guts in thirty-six," I said. My father used to tell me a story about the kulaks, about the collectivization in the Ukraine. "Three million people allowed to starve to death," he had berated a hack at the *Worker* office—one day in thirty-three, I believe it was.

"What do you mean?" the hack had retorted without, as I imagined, even looking up from his typewriter. "It was only one million at the most."

But my mother remembered things differently. "Everyone talked to everyone in the old days, it wasn't like now. Of course Paul was anti-Stalinist. So was everyone else, except the Stalinists of course. That night Nat was the interpreter. He had been to Moscow in the twenties, but he made a lot of mistakes I guess because I could hear them laughing in the other room while I was washing up. Nat told me later that Stalin said, 'With enemies like you I don't need friends,' and your father was terrible, he said 'Just as well you don't need friends, comrade Stalin, since you've killed them all off by now.'"

"And how did Stalin take that?" I asked, amazed at my ignorance of my own family.

"How should I know?" My mother sounded irritated. "He was out of his country, there was nothing he could do. He was just like the rest of Paul's friends. All they wanted was to eat my cooking and borrow money from your father and have him run their errands. . . ." The grudge tone again, taking over. I had to be quick.

"But how did you know it wasn't a joke? It could have been some other eastern European with a black moustache."

"What moustache? You don't think he went around looking like his picture? He had shaved it off. Your father, that was the year he let his moustache grow, looked more like Stalin than Stalin did that night. How do I know for sure? Because two days later Charles—you know what a gentleman he is—called and asked me, 'Did that s.o.b. Stalin behave himself at your place the other night?' Until then I wasn't sure myself. Do you remember that necklace, a string of painted wooden beads I used to have? You always loved them."

"You told me they were Mexican," I accused my mother. Silence maybe, but outright deception? Would I live long enough to rewrite the past in its true colors?

"They were a gift from Stalin. I couldn't tell you that in 1950, could I? And don't you tell Georgina," she ordered me abruptly. The censor was at work again. She began to pile up the tea things and took them out and washed them under water so hot I couldn't stand it, as I found when I brought in the one spoon she had overlooked. It was as though she meant to destroy the last crumb of evidence of her chance confession. The next day she went home to her little apartment east of Union Square, taking the little bag of pebbles she'd collected on the bay. She still has them in the apartment, in a little dish that my father, who had a lethally sweet tooth, kept filled with candy for his own private consumption.

"But are you sure it was thirty-six?" I asked when I phoned her the next evening to make sure she had got home safely. I knew I shouldn't hound her, that she would still be tired after the long hot bus ride. She said it had to be thirty-six because in thirty-five she had just met my father and in thirty-seven she was pregnant with my sister. "I would remember being pregnant because I had only the one maternity dress Ida made me, a flowered dimity I wore all summer. But you're not going to mention it again, are you? Let sleeping dogs lie. Oh, and speaking of sleeping dogs," she went on, in a sudden burst of energy that signaled the announcement of bad news for which she could in no way be held responsible, "Do you know who died? Jim

Reilly. I ran into Bridget in Shopwell last night on my way home from the bus. She didn't let them run an obit in the paper, she didn't want the whole story rehashed in the press." Reilly was a pal of my father's from the old days. In the early fifties he was indicted and nearly went to jail for letting China go Communist.

"Let the dead bury the dead," I said, although I don't usually quote the Bible, least of all to my mother who still hasn't forgiven me for wanting to become a Catholic when we were living in the Bronx across from St. Angela's thirty-five years ago. I was six at the time.

"I never knew what that kind of saying meant," my mother complained. "But it sounds like something I might agree with. I meant to ask you, what does your friend Georgina . . ."

"Georgiana," I corrected her.

"Live on?"

"Other people's leavings," I said, wilfully exaggerating Georgiana's poverty because it pained me to hear my mother assume others enjoyed advantages denied her. Even if such was usually the case. The grudge tone again. "She bought her house in 1942, her clothes are from the Well-fleet thrift shop, she sells an article a year to *Commentary* or something of the sort. Frugal and generous, like you," I added, to soften the reproach. "Anyway, I was thinking, you know, after you left, that it was only fair Stalin got one meal out of you, lemon meringue pie and all. After all, he fed our whole family for years and years." Should I have said that? Would she hang up? After thirty-five years I still couldn't predict my mother's reactions.

"He fed a lot of families, and he still does," she said testily and then shifted with finality into the bright formal mode she prefers, "Tell Peter I said thank you for giving me a real vacation. I don't know anyone who has a son-in-law who would put himself out like that." (He had driven her from Truro to the bus station in Hyannis.) "And thank the girls for letting me share their room."

The scrub pines growing by fits and starts from the poor soil of the outer Cape looked, behind the picture window of our off-season rental, like a diorama at the Museum of Natural History. But the outdoors in its pristine state never looked real to me. What was real was what my mother had told me about the old days. After our phone conversation I sat alone in front of the glass-bound pines and tried to make sense of her hastily suppressed revelation. "Don't say anything to Georgina." My mother had a great superstitious faith in the power of the spoken word, or rather of the word not spoken. If you don't say it, it's not true. As if the truth exposed were a cancer (but she never said "cancer," she said "c") bound to metastasize. I had seen her work her negative magic, her domestic containment policy, on our family, but this was the first time I had ever caught her effectively wishing a history-book dictator out of—if not the history books—at least out of her own life. Mexican beads, indeed. I felt betrayed.

My father—I can hear my mother saying, "It's not something you tell everyone," but I choose for once to ignore the warning—was a professional anti-Stalinist. An expert on what he hated. There were those who paid him for the expertise and those who paid him for the hatred and the latter did him and the rest of us a great deal of harm. That much I understood. What I couldn't figure out, thinking it over that evening, was why he had never told me about his meeting with the man who ruled his life from—but it was no longer quite accurate to say—a distance. They had sat face to face, he and Stalin, in the little cabin in Croton, under the ceiling fan. The Indian summer heat was intense. Outside the crickets chirped to beat the band. There was no liquor, not even beer, in the house because my father didn't drink and never thought to supply his friends with what he had no taste for.

Perhaps in that heat the meeting was less cordial and relaxed than my mother guessed, or would admit. Perhaps there was a terrible row that she missed, with the water running in the kitchen. Perhaps the two men, my father with his wavy hair and full moustache, and Stalin, close cropped and clean shaven, nearly came to blows and had to be torn apart by poor skinny Nat, who had just left the *Worker* and in a few years would be employed by the Dies Committee. Perhaps the sense of purpose, the conviction with which he pursued fellow travelers and comsymps was born that evening or at any rate confirmed, and neither the velvet consistency of the lemon custard nor the gravity-defying meringue in its congealed trembling waves, my mother's peace offering to the world at her doorstep, could prevail against that atmosphere of hatred and gall.

Or, and this is more likely, knowing my father's difficult character, perhaps Stalin made some small offensive gesture, drumming impatiently on the arm of his chair while my father, passionate autodidact, recited his favorite *Invictus* ("My head is bloody, but unbowed") or *The Ballad of Reading Gaol* ("All men kill the thing they love"). Or Stalin may have dropped some offhand remark that bred a resentment too deep for words. This was never so very deep with my poor father, who tortured his family with weeks, even months, of sullen silence when he felt he had been slighted. Forgetting to kiss him goodnight, or declining his invitation to go for a walk after dinner, was enough to launch a cold war at home that thawed only when, under my mother's prodding, I went to his room and apologized. He was quick to come around then, he could sulk but he was also a gossip and missed his homegrown captive audience, and this is why I found it strange that in none of the tête-à-têtes that marked our frequent reconciliations did he ever mention the occasion of which my mother had spoken. It would have been so natural, even in the circumspect and censored fifties, for him to drop a remark.

"When I met Stalin, he was wearing a pair of *huaraches* that stank. The Mexicans tan hides in their own piss. Bernal Diaz reported it first. You've never read Bernal Diaz? There on the bottom shelf, don't mind the dust, all the way to the left, left, that's your right, a daughter of mine should know her left from her right. There, read that, it's an amazing book and you who are studying Spinach will love it."

"I didn't know you met Stalin," I would have backtracked, attentive straightman to my father's routines.

"There are many things you don't know about your old man," he'd have said archly. "Remind me to tell you the story some other time. Now go and see if your poor mother needs you in the kitchen." This would not have been, as with my mother, an evasion, but his way of drawing out the suspense, in keeping with his sense of drama, of self-dramatization.

But nothing of the sort had he said. To be sure we talked about Stalin all the time, in the fifties, when I was a schoolgirl and my father was on the staff of a Senate subcommittee. But the talk was abstract and impersonal, or seemed so to me then. My father lectured me on Stalin's contagious cynicism (the story of the party hack and the kulaks), on the man's stupidity (the Lysenko episode), his brutality. Until I was sick of hearing about Stalin, dead or alive, and accused my father of playing up the Soviet dictator's influence in order to enhance his own. That bit of insubordination earned me six months of my father's silence. He would cross the street, if need be, to avoid greeting me. And after we got back on speaking terms, things were not as before. He never mentioned his—I nearly said "beloved"—Stalin again in my hearing.

Instead of sulking my father should have told me about the summer of thirty-six. Why had he kept it to himself? The pine trees of extreme New England with their greedy hidden roots and light exposed branches were of no help to me. "Don't say anything to Georgina." My mother's warning was naïve, I now saw. Georgiana probably knew as much or more than my mother did about Stalin's visit to the United States at the time of the Popular Front. No doubt she too, my friend, had suppressed the truth. In her book dealing with the upheavals of the sixties she denounces Stalin's insularity, his "wilful ignorance of the non-Soviet world he was to visit only as an old man surrounded by bodyguards and flunkies." Unquote. And if Georgiana could suppress the truth, couldn't others as well? What if a whole generation of Stalin haters and Stalin supporters had conspired in some way to keep back the facts? Imagine a conspiracy of silence linking the pros and the antis, forming a secret bond among them even in the days of their most virulent set-tos. Many sweeping accusations were made during the Cold War, but no one ever accused a former associate of having had Stalin home to dinner in Boston or Baltimore. The very absence in all the literature of anything to corroborate my mother's story (a story she, whose lies were all of omission, would have been incapable of inventing) proved the existence of this conspiracy of silence.

What mischief had Stalin perpetrated on the east coast of the United States in 1936? If only one knew, it might explain much that continued to puzzle us. Why my father had stopped speaking to his best friend Charles, during the Vietnam War. Why, at the forty-fifth reunion of my mother's college class (Hunter '36), the Young People's Socialist League girls and the Young Communist League alumnae were still giving one another the cold shoulder. And who knows, perhaps it would turn out that like an evil Johnny Appleseed Stalin had come to our shores only to sow the seeds that blossomed, long after his death, into what we call the neoconservative movement.

I had to know more. My mother couldn't, or wouldn't, tell me. Georgiana, who reached the States via London only in 1940, was not, despite everything, a reliable source. Who else was there? I drew up a long list of possible informants. The word is neutral in anthropology but ugly in politics. Could I deal with the latter as a branch of the former? I saw that if I wanted to pursue the question, I would have to give up my children for adoption, abandon my husband, and devote myself exclusively to the search. It would be like returning to the womb, to chaos, to the heart of one of my father's long silences.

Back in the city in October, I showed the list to my mother one night after dinner.

"Give me a pencil," she said, and wet the lead between her lips and made a mark next to every other name. "These are all gone, dear," she said, as if to break the news gently. "I see you don't read the *Times* as carefully as I do. Jones died last week. He published that awful magazine. Did I tell you how they kept sending me notices to renew the subscription? I finally wrote them, 'My husband is dead but if he were alive he would have nothing to do with you.' That shut them up. You know Paul never voted Republican after Eisenhower. Where did you get these names? What a memory you have, just like your father. But if you've got your heart set on it, you could talk to Charles. I don't think he'd mind."

It was Charles who, according to my mother, had phoned after the dinner in Croton to ask, "Did that s.o.b. Stalin behave himself?" Perhaps with some gentle prodding he might remember what my mother had replied.

At the time my father died he had not spoken to Charles in nearly ten years. But when Charles saw the obit in the *Times* he wrote my mother a note and later he arranged the sale, to an Ohio university, of my father's library (described in Charles's catalogs as "a rare collection of pamphlets and ephemera of the American labor movement, dating back to the 1920s"). At one time Charles's shop was on Fourth Avenue. Now he did only a mail order book business from a loft on lower Broadway. And even that was run mostly by a younger assistant. He came to work only two mornings a week. I arranged to meet him at the loft on one of his mornings in.

I wasn't sure, once I was there, how I ought to bring the conversation round to the subject that obsessed me. I felt ill at ease with Charles, unassuming good-natured little man though he was. I could remember too many of my father's unkind barbs at his expense. My father looked down on Charles because he had remained an observer, a collector, an archivist of his times, declining to take his chances in the arena. Charles's name was not in the index of any of the thousands of books on his hundreds of shelves. My father's, with one or two page references, figured in at least a dozen.

I was amazed to see how Charles's business had grown. American radical movements were one thing, but where had he come by the autograph of Hitler that hung over his desk?

"My assistant picked that up at auction last month," he anticipated my question. He had always had the thin piping voice of an old man. "I won't have any trouble getting rid of it. Hitler is big this year."

"What about Stalin," I seized the occasion. "I don't suppose you have his autograph too, or that there'd be a demand for it."

"Funny you should ask." Charles went to a filing cabinet and opened it just a crack, as if to conceal the contents from me, or maybe he was just conserving his strength. An old man, eighty at least. My father would have been eighty if he had lived. Stalin would have been a hundred and six. God is merciful.

"Go ahead, take it, it won't bite you." Charles handed me what was apparently a menu from a Village restaurant whose name was unknown to me. It was an old menu. Under the list of beverages—cherry crush, real ginger ale, priced at five cents and under—was a scrawl in Cyrillic. I could decipher it; my father had taught me the Russian alphabet. It was a man's name. Dzhugashvili.

"Where did you get this?"

"It was among your father's junk," he said. My father was a man who clipped articles and reviews and stuck them inside books and forgot about them. He saved flyers, menus, tickets, campaign buttons. But why did Charles call it junk? Did he think I was going to question the price he had obtained for my father's library? As if I cared about converting lost time into found money. I had other worries.

"Could it be authentic?" Now was his chance to tell me the whole story. I was sure he had it all inside his bare speckled skull. He cleared a corner of his desk for me to sit, and dropped into the stuffed chair behind it. His hands fumbled as if looking for some familiar object and then he said apologetically, "I don't smoke the pipe anymore. I gave it up when Molly was so sick."

Molly was his second wife, who had died the year before. It was two years at least since I had last seen Charles. I ought to have acknowledged his loss at the outset. Stalin was destroying my humanity too.

"I still remember the summer I worked in the shop," I said. "She was such fun to work for. She taught me how to tie a slip knot. One of the most useful things I learned that year." I laid the menu on the desk where he couldn't miss it, in case his mind had wandered.

"You'd like to know if it's real," Charles said after a pause that would have allowed time to suck at a pipe. "Trouble is, I don't know anyone who can appraise it for us." He thought my mind was on business, on commerce. He was used to ministering to his customers' follies. "And let's say it was real, we'd still have to explain, to any prospective buyer, the provenance, who it was carried a Village menu around Moscow with him way back when."

"I can't imagine," I said.

Charles took the time not to smoke his pipe. "Some groupie, some poor s.o.b. What do we do with it? Take it if you like. See what you can do with it. I don't have time at my age for purely speculative ventures." He laughed his high-pitched laugh, like a bat's if one could hear them.

"That's very kind of you," I said. Was it? If I accepted this bit of evidence I would spend the rest of my life trying to establish just what it was evidence of. Stalin would rule me with his dead hand, as he had ruled my father and countless millions.

"You're too generous, Charles." I slid off the desk. "I couldn't accept. You've done so much for our family already." I looked him in the eye, which wasn't easy as his eyes were guarded by a pair of thick lenses. "But I understand what you're saying. I was born too late to get in on the secret."

If he winked at me from behind those shining convex sentries I'll never know either.

The Shoe Clerk

I worked in a shoe store. I sold shoes. I spent half my time kneeling at the customers' feet and the other half climbing tall ladders in the stockroom. The work was tiring but not excessively so. I didn't mind handling feet. Call them stupid if you like. They are also tough, alert, and democratic. There is no fat on them and they put up with a lot.

The store had two vast corner windows on one of the city's most elegant streets. Hundreds of thousands of well-fed and well-clothed people passed that corner every week on their way to gratification or disappointment or the coffee shops on the narrow side streets. You may think that I would have felt trapped inside my glass cage, watching those crowds free to come and go. In fact I considered that I had the advantage of a stationary vantage point while they, poor folk, were on the run. I was a follower of Epicurus who preached not, as is often thought, the mad pursuit of pleasure (unthinkable before modern hygiene and the discovery of antibiotics) but the minimization of pain. The less you want the less they can hurt you. Limit your desires, was his advice. I mention the Greek philosopher only to show that my humility had solid classical antecedents.

One day the king of X came into the shop with his wife.

16

In those days he visited our country once a year, took two floors in the best hotel, shopped for a new wardrobe, saw his doctors and friends. I waited on his wife, the queen, as I would have on any customer requiring half a dozen pairs of alligator pumps.

"That's a bit of Figaro you're whistling," she remarked as I was tying the parcel.

"I'm sorry, Madam, I wasn't aware . . ."

"Oh, don't apologize, it seems appropriate to the setting. You don't mind my saying that?" she asked with charming condescension. Of course I didn't mind.

Neither did I mind when two days later I received at home her invitation to visit X as the guest of the royal family. At the bottom of the card she had written, *"Pour cet air de Mozart que vous siffliez en me chaussant."* On my next vacation from the shop, I went to X.

Before the war the kingdom of X had its own airline, one plane for each hemisphere of the globe. I changed planes in Hong Kong and from there it was only a short flight to the capital, where I spent two weeks in a hilltop villa overlooking the harbor. I had expected elephant rides and visits to jungle ruins. Instead the queen slyly presented me with a violin, quite a decent instrument, and asked me to accompany her. I was once what is known as a serious musician. I gave it up for reasons I could never make clear to my teachers or even, I'm afraid, to myself. To play duets with the queen of X, whose lowered eyelids were as round as the keys on her silver flute, was a pleasure mixed with some pain, yet I bore it gladly for her sake.

During those two weeks in X I saw the king only twice. Once at breakfast he dropped by long enough to assure me that each of the beggars who knelt by the palace gates by day went home at night to the bosom of a loving and prosperous family.

"But their infirmities?" I insisted.

"Mere professional deformation," he answered with a sly smile. On my last evening in X he informed me that he was about to receive a large delegation from my own country. Would I like to be introduced, he wondered, or would I rather, just for the fun of it, that he adopt me for the evening as one of his subjects? I could scarcely refuse the offer of adoption from a king. As in X it is considered rude to meet an interlocutor's gaze, I had only to keep my green eyes averted throughout the evening.

I was thus at liberty to observe the delegation from my country. Our minister of culture was leading a group into the jungle to inspect ruins of the late classical period. There was one small gem of a temple, he confessed, that was keeping him awake nights. He wondered if the king would permit our country to pay for its restoration?

My borrowed sovereign smiled.

"Of course," the minister then added, "we would have to remove it from its present site for some time. I thought five years for the restoration and perhaps fifteen for display. Millions would see it. It would revitalize your tourist industry, you know."

"If only we had one," the king sighed. "I find it admirable that your great nation in its present period of empire is so modest it prefers to restore the monuments of former epochs rather than build its own. Yet how can I accept your gracious offer? Some of my people worship at this temple that has caught your eye. They would not forgive me if I were to remove it from their care. They have so little else besides."

From beneath lowered eyelids I had been watching our ambassador to X. His own eyes darted from left to right with animal alertness. Now he attacked. "When was that little number built? A thousand years ago? By now it's in the public domain as we say. You can't just let it rot away."

The king answered quickly. "With your great experience of international affairs you will have noticed by now that when the treasure is in our own backyard we take a narrow viewpoint. When it's in the neighbor's yard, well, one invokes the brotherhood of man." He held up his two empty hands to show he was unarmed.

"But twenty years is nothing," the ambassador insisted.

"In your own country," the king said, "that is of course true. But here in X I'm afraid we do not live as long as you giants of the earth—why here twenty years may be half a lifetime. Who knows, in twenty years I myself may no longer be king. . . . So much can happen in twenty years."

He spoke coquettishly but it was clear he meant this to be his last word on the subject. The ambassador took his cue and proposed a toast to the king's health and long reign. When he had drunk, his damp tongue sat on his lower lip like a toad on a stone and his eyes continued to sweep the table from right to left, left to right, like searchlights.

Six months later the king of X was in bitter exile, his country plunged into a cruel civil war fomented by our new foreign minister, who was none other than the ambassador I had watched bait the king at his own table. The papers were suddenly full of this important man's picture and his speeches. I read them looking in vain for some connection between his cumbersome speech—his thoughts had the syntactical force of a neutron bomb, eliminating verbs but not nouns—and the charming country I had visited, where even the beggar went home at night to the bosom of his family. Our new foreign minister preached a doctrine of necessary evil that was no less a doctrine, a piece of perverse theology, for being couched in the bland jargon of an inter-office memorandum. While it might have been admirable in a foxhole under fire, I found his resignation in the face of death repugnant under the circumstances. He was resigned to seeing many others die that he and his ilk might go on living in comfort. He ate and slept and had his picture taken while the kingdom of X on the other side of the globe became a land of homeless beggars. Reading the man's speeches I lost my philosophy. I began to dream of revenge.

What form would it take? I thought of the fairy tales

I had loved as a child with their wonderful reversals, the ennobling of orphans and tailors, the humbling of haughty princes. I wished to arrange something of the sort for this man. A year as delivery boy in our shop, for example, would have done him some good. In our time, of course, fairy tale reversals have often been arranged on a massive scale. We call it revolution. That was not what I had in mind. Something more modest in scope, more economic of means, more accurate of aim, was called for.

When the new foreign minister walked into the shop one day during lunch hour I recognized him at once. I was alone with him for a full fifteen minutes while a limousine waited outside, double parked, the motor running.

"I'll want the usual adjustments," he muttered to me while examining a pair of three hundred dollar Italian loafers. Now that he stood beside me I saw he was rather on the short side, plump and well-dressed of course. His hair had grayed and his ears were small and pointed.

"I beg your pardon," I said, careful not to let on that I knew him. It was the shop's policy to respect the incognito of our celebrated customers.

"The usual adjustments to the internal structure, damn it. Lifts. I want lifts in a pair like this."

"Very good, sir. They'll be ready tomorrow."

"What's wrong with today?"

"There's a small extra charge for rush orders."

"Don't bother me with such details. Don't you know who I am?" he asked, amused at my mortal simplicity. I chose not to reply.

"I've seen you somewhere, you know," he persisted, "which means you've seen me. Did you ever work for . . ." He named a colleague at the ministry."

"We met in X," I said.

"This isn't right, you know. I'm a busy man. I shouldn't have to pump you like this. I'm sure your employer would agree."

So, while slipping a shoehorn between the heel of his left foot and the expensive shoe, I explained how I had come to sit opposite him at the king's table in X.

He strode back and forth on the carpet in front of the low mirror, lifting his trousers from the knee to admire the new shoes.

"Are they comfortable?" I asked. I always asked that.

"Very," he said. "But you're not a shoe salesman," he suddenly accused. If he had been in the right his angry blast would have made me cringe.

"I'm sorry if the customer is in any way dissatisfied," I said mildly.

"Perfectly satisfied," he shouted. "That's what's so uncanny. You fit in here just as you fit at the court of X. You're like wallpaper." He sat down and allowed me to remove the new shoes and tie the laces on his old ones for him. I gave them a wipe with a rag while I was at it.

"It will be a long time before one visits X again," I said while buffing.

He grunted and said, "Too bad about the king. Damn foolish of him, trying to play both ends against the middle. Still I expect he'll manage to die in his bed of old age." He stood up abruptly and his knee almost knocked me in the chin.

"What days are you free?" he asked.

"Sundays and Tuesdays."

"Good, call me Tuesday at this number and we'll see."

He handed me his card with a severe dignity the king of X would have been incapable of assuming.

Trouble had entered my life. For the first time in many years I suffered from insomnia. I could no more imagine what the minister wanted with me than I could admit what I hoped for from him. The following Tuesday at eleven exactly I phoned the number he'd given me. When a voice informed me that the minister was out of town, I felt a sharper pang of disappointment than I could countenance in myself. I was about to flee the apartment in disgust when the phone rang. A warm female voice told me to hold for the minister. His deep growl shook me.

"I'm leaving for the airport in half an hour. I'll pick you up and we'll talk en route. The chauffeur will drop you back in town." He hung up. There had been no time to say yes or no, much less to furnish my address. But he had not needed to ask for it.

"I suppose you're wondering where I'm off to," he began with weary impatience. The black limousine was as comfortable inside as one's own bed at bedtime, but the minister sat upright and alert, as if he didn't quite trust his driver or me either. Having invited me to sit next to him he wanted nevertheless to mark the difference between us. Therefore I replied with caution.

"I had no intention of asking. Men may confide in their barber but seldom in a shoe salesman."

"Ah, and why is that, do you suppose?" he asked without bothering to look my way. His eye was on the road.

"When a man sits immobilized, facing his mirror image for an hour, he needs to remind himself that he is something more than the collection of features staring him in the face. He has been places, done things, formed opinions. In my line of work of course it's quite different. The mirrors start at the floor and end at the knee." I felt a fool telling him all this. What did he care about my line of work?

"I see," he said. "Why did you not become a barber then? You might pick up more information at any rate. It would be more intellectually rewarding, I should think," he added drily. I was aware that I was being bullied. I had read that he bullied his colleagues at the ministry. No doubt it was required in his line of work.

"Sir," I replied mildly, "the kind of information men might choose to share with their barber is of no interest to me. To tell the truth I enjoy my work because I deal, as you might say, with dumb creatures, feet I mean. And while I try to serve them conscientiously I am free meanwhile to pursue my own thoughts."

"Ah, your own thoughts. Tell me, what do you think about while you're lacing shoes?"

"As you are neither my barber nor my shoe salesman I shall not burden you with that information," I replied.

"What discretion, what aptitude," he exclaimed. "No wonder the king of X fell for you. Ah, sorry, it was the king's wife, wasn't it? Sure you won't have a drink?" I declined to serve myself from the bar built into the back of the front seat.

We had reached the long gloomy boulevard leading to the airport. A light rain had begun to fall but inside the car we sat as in an English drawing room at tea time. The chauffeur behind his gray plush curtain might have been a giant rat with handsome whiskers, for all one could see of him. The minister had sought to give offense. He was inciting rebellion so that he could then put me in my place. I already knew my place.

"I'm afraid you greatly overestimate my powers of attraction," I said, taking up his remark about the queen, but his mind was already elsewhere.

"The chauffeur will let you off where you like. Of course you'll ride up front with him on the way back. You won't mind?"

"As you like," I said, unwittingly passing the last hurdle of my test. For his next words were these:

"As one of my staff it seems more appropriate. We want to start you off on good terms with your colleagues."

"My colleagues?" I was startled.

"Of course," he said, enjoying the advantage I'd given him at last. "You don't suppose I'd waste my time like this unless I was serious about you. I've been meaning to recruit a valet, a man's man—what is the word you use these days—since I took office. We know you travel well and since I expect to be doing a great deal of traveling you'll do as well as anyone. You'll start Sunday, so clear up any business of your own before then. And complete discretion of course. You won't find that difficult."

All I could think at that moment was that I owed the honor, if such it was, to my slight stature. I was about the same height as the minister but weighed perhaps forty pounds less. Next to me he would never feel dwarfed.

"Now, one more question and we're there," he said as the car turned off the boulevard at a sign marked simply PRIVATE. "Why did you never marry?"

"Why do you ask?" It was a stupid question, as he made me feel at once.

"Why do I ask? Because if I hire a man I want to know he's going to be loyal. Do you think I give a hoot in hell about your private life?"

"No, of course not . . ."

"Well then."

"I-I was young . . ." I stuttered, "when events forced me to leave Germany. My parents stayed behind and perished. After two years in England, a school, an internment camp, I went to an uncle in Mexico, my mother's older brother. My cousins adapted quickly to the local custom, married young and had many children, relieving me of the obligation, so to speak. . . ."

"You have no accent," he said. Of the whole narration, so painful to me, he had fixed on this point. How little I understood him yet.

"I lost it somehow," I muttered. In fact it was beaten out of me on the playing fields of England. Some of those fields were ringed with barbed wire.

"But your parents were cultured people? What you Germans call *Bildung,* that's what I'm after. C'mon, name me five contemporaries of Alexander the Great."

"His teacher Aristotle," I began, "his father Philip of Macedon, his gadfly Diogenes the Cynic, his good friend Cleitus whom he killed in a drunken row, the Persian king Darius Codomannus whom he . . ."

"Enough, enough. There you see what I'm after. I could have hired some Mexican or Filipino . . ."

"Perhaps you would like time to consider your generous offer."

"Haven't got the time. We're going to China next week." The limousine had pulled to a stop. "I'll expect you Sunday," he said as I held the door open for him, under the jealous eye of the chauffeur, who was not after all a gray rat but a heavyset Irishman by the look of him.

"Very good, sir," I said as the minister nodded and rushed past me unseeing. I was already his man.

At the shoe store I simply told them that my Mexican uncle had died and I was going down to see the estate. No one seemed to mind my leaving on short notice. My boss even insisted on giving me a pair of black oxfords faded from long exposure in the shop window. I accepted the gift gratefully and left the store like any customer, with a package under my arm, and took my place in the crowd I had often studied from behind the plate glass window. I had no other farewells to make before leaving for the capital. Vera, my sometime mistress, was in Japan just then or was it Thailand, on the last lap of a tour with her husband, the noted orchestra leader Incessu. I knew how busy she would be on her return. It might be months before she noticed my absence.

And thus I entered into domestic service with our foreign minister, referred to hereinafter as the F.M. You may wonder why in our democratic and mechanized society any man, even a cabinet member, would require the services of a valet. The answer lay in our man's vast and vastly celebrated ambition. Although his speeches measured the weight of history and the pressure of existing institutions, although he professed a deep skepticism as to what any one man could accomplish in a single lifetime, in practice the F.M. never met a man he could trust to do the job in his place. He had to be everywhere at once and see to it all for himself. Monday Pakistan, Tuesday China, Friday Korea, Saturday the Philippines. He had no time to pack a bag or dicker with hotel laundries. The empire to which he aspired for our country depended on him alone and he depended, I may say, on me.

I took to my duties like a fish to water or, as the Chinese poet says, like a guerrilla army to the countryside. My training in the shoe store stood me in good stead, as did a number of little tricks and *tournemains* I remembered from my childhood in the capital of *Wohnkultur*. Ways of folding a handkerchief elegantly or removing the lint from a pair of trousers in a hurry. The moustache that became a part of the F.M.'s persona was my idea, for, of course I became his barber and tailor in time, and even his masseur.

After sitting erect in a stiff-bottomed chair through long negotiations with the Soviets, he was happy to submit his tired, overfed body to my patient hands. He settled himself belly down on a Louis XV marquetry table where the Czar Alexander had once laid out his games of patience.

"Our children will thank me for what I've accomplished today," the F.M. sighed as I began to knead his quiet flesh. "Pity neither of us has any. Oh well, and that draft bill will have to be rammed through now."

"Will it, sir?" He welcomed my questions on such occasions. They allowed him to leak information to the eavesdropping Russians that was to be withheld from the public at home.

"Sure. Why is it so hard for people to understand that if you want peace, you prepare for war."

"I thought this method had been tried and found wanting," I permitted myself to observe to the small of his back.

"That's how it may look from where you stand," he said, "but from my vantage point"—eyes shut, face down on a wooden table—"it's a whole new ballgame." He favored baseball slang in Moscow. It slowed the interpreters during difficult negotiations and left him more time to prepare his next move.

"What means this, ballgame?" I chaffed him. He loved that.

"C'mon, we'd all like to pack up and go home and sit on our hands but it ain't in the cards. . . ." He also affected this kind of down-home patter with the Russians, who countered by tossing off cryptic proverbs.

"We've got the bomb, right?" he went on. "And they've got the bomb. So far so good." I let my silence pass for assent. "Okay, now this bomb is strictly a weapon of last resort. On that we all agree."

"As in 1945?" I asked.

"Ah, that feels good, you found the spot. No, Hiroshima was an exceptional case. That was the only time the bomb was used in a purely symbolic way. From then on, of course, it went on to become the only game in town. While your conventional weapons—your dynamite, your nerve gas, anthrax, napalm, what have you—have taken on a strictly symbolic function. It's a Barnum and Bailey world, we can thank our lucky stars for that. Of course this goes for manpower as well. Which means you simply can't keep the peace these days without a standing army of several million. Let's say we agree not to deploy any more missiles in Europe. That's a real concession. At the same time, we have to be able to call up two hundred thousand men. A purely symbolic threat. The gain is clear."

"Will they think so?"

"The Russkies? That's the only language they understand."

"I see, sir. I meant the young men, the draftees. . . ."

"Hang it." He sat up. I handed him a hot towel. "Compared to the bomb what's two years under conventional combat conditions. Why it's"—he sought a choice bit of slang—"a piece of cake."

To die is bad enough and will happen to us all. But to die a symbolic death and still to rot in the ground with no mourners—this is something even my wretched parents were spared. They were told that being Jews they did not deserve to live. Their right to existence was questioned but not their existence itself. Is that splitting hairs? All empires are not alike. The F.M. reasoned inversely, so to speak. He did not question the right of the people of X (or Y, or later Z) to go on planting their rice each spring. But once they interfered with his grand design for world order he relegated them with a wave of his hand (I was there, I saw him wave it) to a merely symbolic function within his schema. They had ceased to exist for him. They were already as good as dead.

I should have stayed in the shoe store. It was peaceful there, the floors were carpeted throughout, not just in front of the little mirrors, and neither I nor the customers were called, on those premises, to tasks too great for us. With the F.M., on the contrary, I suffered a professional deformation parallel to his own. He was obsessed with the international balance of terror. I was obsessed with his stupidity. He was responsible for the continuation of human history or its permanent interruption. I was responsible for his health and comfort. Comfort and terror. By virtue of my position I was tortured, like no one else on earth, by this paradox. Under torture I gave way. Also, since childhood I had been subject to sudden consuming rages, tantrums was too small a word even then, seizures more like it. My mother blamed the *Kristallnacht,* but I am quite sure this choleric streak of mine was far more ancient in origin. I am only a man and there is much I do not understand.

One night, when the F.M. lay in bed with a bad cold and I had just brought in his second hot toddy of the evening, he asked me to plump up the pillows for him. I had done it many times before, but this time I had to excuse myself and run to my room behind the kitchen and shut the door. I wept, I moaned, and then I stood up and berated my own stupidity. Living in dependence had dulled my wits but freedom was within my grasp. To release myself from the paradox I had only to remove both terms at once by destroying their embodiment, my master. Would he appreciate the symbolism of that? I would soon find out.

The jejune existence that had been my lot till then would

work in my favor, would receive in fact its vindication. I had given no hostages to fortune. Neither wife nor friend nor child need ever suffer the consequences of my deed. That week of preparation was the most feverishly excited of my life. I set a date: the following Thursday night when the rest of the household staff would be out. As for the method, my classical background, so prized by the F.M., furnished a scenario. I began to sharpen a letter opener I owned that looked like a small dagger. I wondered if the F.M. would have the presence of mind, as it entered him below the left nipple, to mutter, "*Et tu*, Max?" So be it.

On the fateful Thursday morning the F.M. complained his favorite shoes were pinching his feet. He was growing a corn on his little left toe. "You'll go down to the shop and pick up another pair," he said casually. I would do nothing of the sort. I had other plans for that day. The chauffeur agreed to run the errand for me. He returned with the parcel and left on his night out.

I was sitting in my room late that evening, reading the Bible, when the F.M. came in. He had not bothered to knock. I closed the book, marking the page with the paperknife I'd been honing all week, and stood to face him.

"What kind of joke is this?" he bellowed. "These shoes are two sizes too small." He was livid. I was pale. I asked to see the shoes and showed him the size marking. I said the shoes had probably been mismarked but that I would look into the matter in the morning. To my amazement I was able to say "in the morning" without the trace of a stammer.

"Ah, the morning. What kind of stalling tactic is that? I hear it all day at work and in my own home even the servants throw it up to me. Look into the matter. In this town even the shoeshine boys talk like bureaucrats."

"I was wrong to entrust the errand to the chauffeur," I said coolly. After a week on fire I was now a block of ancient ice. Greatness was within my grasp.

"And why in God's name did you send that idiot? I suppose you think you're too important now to bother with a pair of shoes. That was not always the case. I should have left you where I found you, on your knees." He screamed in my ear and I backed away, wondering if his voice carried as far as the apartment of the secret service on the floor below. Anyway, I thought bitterly, the whole house was probably bugged from top to bottom. If I slew the monster then and there the world would be sure to mistake my motive, call it an act of personal vengeance. And perhaps the world would be right. Was I a budding tyrannicide or only an aggrieved houseboy? The sight of that paperknife with its lethal cutting edge mocked me. I threw it away. I told myself I could have slain a giant, like David. I could not bring myself to topple a pygmy.

The next morning the F.M. made no allusion to our scene or rather he acknowledged it by insisting I take a week's vacation, effective at once. I took the bus due north. I preferred it to the plane. I didn't want to ride with the horde of gray men in gray suits who would remind me of everything I was fleeing. Serving the F.M. was like living on a heavier, slow-moving planet. It was only when I had escaped from his pull that I could judge what a compressed existence I led around him. I resolved during the long bus ride to resign from his service. What perverse loyalty prevented me from doing so?

Vera could have helped me but Vera didn't know the truth. In the city where I had formerly worked I took a hotel room and phoned her, told her I was just up from Mexico. She agreed to meet me the following afternoon. To contain my agitation I reminded myself that her interest in me was directly proportional to the interval between encounters. It was nearly a year since our last meeting. I came early to the appointed place but apparently she had come even earlier, and to hide the fact was walking away up the avenue when I arrived. I would have been happy to follow her for hours through the city streets. For as long as I could keep her in sight I was a free man with a future no more illusory than anyone else's, only, perhaps, a good deal shorter. That afternoon I measured the future in minutes and seconds.

"This reminds me of my student days in Paris," she said after lunch when we returned to the rather shabby hotel. She plied me with questions about my life in Mexico and appeared to listen to my answers but soon interrupted me saying, "You've changed, Max." It was an opinion without appeal. Vera was born into a family of musicians and physicists. Although she was neither, no one who knew her doubted she could have been either or both if she had chosen. She had what is called natural authority even if, as now, she was often wrong.

"Have I? In what way?" I asked.

"You were always maddeningly reticent, one knew that about you. It was a relief from the rest of them. You didn't advertise. But now you're positively furtive. I'm not sure I like it."

"Perhaps we should have gone somewhere more public," I offered. "The zoo, the planetarium."

"The planetarium," she said. "My father used to take me there once a year. I'm sure they've spoiled it by now with their close-ups of Jupiter. There's no mystery any more," she went on, echoing an editorial that had run the day before in the local paper. "The planets have lost their privacy like everything else. I mean, don't you find it revolting when they interview public figures sitting at home in shirt-sleeves like some shopkeeper going over his books in the back of the store. So *wulgar*."

"I hadn't thought of it," I said. "Yet if you object to secrecy . . ."

"They don't all lend themselves of course." She pursued her own train of thought, a voluble tease. "Our new foreign minister is obviously different. You always see him correctly dressed."

"Do you?"

"Oh yes, Vlado met him, you know, when he was playing in the capital."

"What did he make of him?" I asked, genuinely intrigued to know what Vera's husband, no fool, thought of my employer.

"He was impressed despite himself. But he said he could tell from his speech, you know, that tired monotone, that he must be tone deaf."

"You can't have everything," I said pointedly.

"Oh Max, do you mind my mentioning Vlado? It must be the Mexican influence. You never used to be jealous. I thought that was one of the things you liked about me, my being my father's daughter and Vlado's wife. I come with several pedigrees . . ."

"Shut up."

"I won't." She drew away from me. "Apologize at once."

"I'm sorry," I said. "Go on about Vlado and the foreign minister."

"Yes, well, Max you're such a child. Don't look so glum. We're still friends. You're the one who's gone off, you know, south of the border. I may come to visit you one of these days on your finca. You actually grow coffee?"

"Yes," I said. "It's still quite primitive. When will you come?"

"Soon," she said guiltily. It was one thing to tell lies but I had no business wringing false promises from her. "Anyway," she changed the subject, "I am glad you're out of that awful shoe store. You have done some odd things in your time. Vlado says you could have played with a decent orchestra or even made a career as a soloist with luck. But after you walked out on your debut . . . Whatever possessed you? To work so hard for years and give it all up to clerk in a shop?"

"It was a very high-class establishment, you may recall. Our customers were drawn from the elite of several continents."

"Snob," she said. "But all the same to let your talent, your training go up in smoke like that . . ."

"Worse things have happened. I could as easily have gone up in smoke myself with the rest of them. . . ."

"Oh, how I hate your *Mitteleuropa* gallows humor. Like stale smoke in a seminar room. Besides you oughtn't to talk like that. Guilt feelings are destructive." Every American knows such things without reading the papers.

"History is destructive," I quoted the F.M. in one of his rare philosophic moments. "Men are destructive."

"Good, let's hear you get angry for once."

"Anger is destructive," I said and leaned over her, intercepting her view of the low ceiling. But Vera had to have the last word, before she would let me kiss her.

"You haven't changed much, after all. I can still read you like an open book."

At the end of the week I returned to the F.M.'s service, still intending to give notice. I never had the chance.

He greeted me, looking up from the morning's cables: "What took you so long? Pack my bags at once. I'm taking you home to Germany." That night we flew to Wiesbaden where a motorcade awaited to escort us to Frankfurt. I rode in a van with secretaries and communications experts, half listening to their chatter about football scores and shopping opportunities. This was my first trip to Germany since I had been sent off as a child in thirty-eight. I was safe now, ludicrously safe, with my valid passport and an armed escort. Yet I felt uneasy, as if time, like a carpet not tacked to the floor, could slide backward under me at any moment. The van, making slow progress through the morning fog off the Main, could just as easily have been on its way to a collection point for shipment east.

That evening a mob of demonstrators gathered at the chancellor's residence in Bonn, where it had been given out that the F.M. was staying. In our suite at the Parkhotel in Frankfurt he watched them on TV for a moment and then snapped off the set. He settled himself on a glass and chrome Modernstil table for his massage.

"Close your eyes," I suggested when he complained it made him dizzy to look down through the glass. I was about to lay hold of his flesh when something grabbed me from behind. I was thrown to the floor. I heard the sound of breaking glass, felt a sharp blow to the skull, and passed out.

You have read about the kidnapping. Two movies, half a dozen books, innumerable articles, and a Senate investigation resulted. None mentioned me. I am writing this to complete the record. When I came to, the F.M. was hunched over me, shaking me by the shoulders.

"I'm cold," he said. Naturally enough, for he was still naked and we were, I saw, sitting up and rubbing my eyes, in a kind of basement bunker, perhaps a bomb shelter from the last war. The ceiling, some eight feet up, was of concrete with a metal door set in the center. The edges of the door were outlined in light but down below we sat in darkness. As I had the good fortune to be wearing my pajamas I gave the top to the F.M. Once he had tied it around his middle, he stood up, and with all the ferocious energy that made him the admiration of his friends and the terror of his enemies, he announced, "This is war. Dig a latrine."

Although I could have disobeyed with no great consequence I did as I was told for the moment. I had got up a few handfuls of dirt when he quit his nervous pacing and said, "Stop that rodent scratching. I have something important to say."

"Sir?"

"There's one thing I want settled right away while we're in full possession of our faculties. Whoever holds out longer has the right to dispose of the other's remains. The first goal of the statesman is survival."

"Yes, sir." I was astounded. If our unknown captors' plan was to leave us to die of starvation, the F.M. had the advantage over me of a good forty pounds of stored fat and muscle. We both knew this. Why then bother to secure my permission, in advance, to cannibalize my dead body? Had the man suddenly developed a conscience? That was the astonishing point and only the terror could explain it.

But conscience is what subjugates the strong to the weak and no one knew this better than the F.M. He quickly reasserted his authority by adding, "And when we get out of here, I'll see you get a medal for bravery."

"Don't want a medal, sir. What I would like is . . ."

"*Halts Maul,*" a voice bellowed from the lighted region above us. The trap door opened and our captors fell between us like a two-headed *deus ex machina*. Two pairs of legs, two monstrous bodies covered from head to hips in potato sacks with slits for the eyes. Two rifles, trained on the F.M. and me. The burlap bags gave these intruders the look of actors in some drama where the personality has been abolished as a bourgeois excrescence.

"We got a discount," one of the bags said in German. "Two for the price of one. Who are you?"

"I work at the hotel," I said, imitating as best I could his own slurred Frankfurt speech. "I'm a barber, masseur, I give manicures, pedicures, everything gentlemen want, in their rooms."

"What were you doing in his room in your pajamas, old goat?"

"They call me at all hours," I said. "I live at the hotel. I get room and board and tips when I'm lucky. This time I wasn't lucky."

The F.M. looked as if he had something to say but the guard slapped his backside with the muzzle of his rifle.

"How long do I have to sit down here, gentlemen?" I asked. "It's cold, you know."

"That's not up to us," the guard said. "If his friends think he's worth a billion dollars there'll be no trouble."

"A billion," I gasped. "No one is worth that."

"Then he's done for. But if you're his barber you must have murdered his kind many times over in your thoughts. As a member of an oppressed class your reasons for hating him are objectively as valid as ours. We may even give you the honor of executing him. What do you say?"

"Nothing against, gentlemen. But you put me in an awkward position with him. He's already threatened me, you know. He has a foul temper."

"All right, if he bothers you again trim his toenails with this." My guard reached under his burlap and took out a knife. "A little social experiment. Of course if you get hurt it's your own fault, understand?" He handed me the knife, broader and shorter of blade than the dagger I had so recently discarded.

"Barbers know how to care for their blades," I said.

"Then look sharp." And they hoisted themselves back up through the trap door and slammed it over us. The darkness seemed gloomier than before. The F.M. found his voice at last.

"Brilliant," he hissed. "You have to admit I knew what I was doing when I hired you. They won't dare touch us," he gloated, suddenly full of confidence. "We have two hundred fifty thousand troops on German soil. Think of the international consequences. But give me the knife just in case. It's always best to negotiate from a position of strength."

"No," I said softly. "I won't." It was the first time I had ever refused an order to his face. Perhaps that's why he didn't even notice at first.

"Sickening pair, weren't they," he continued. "But you should have asked them for something to eat. I'm famished."

"Here, you can start with this." I shoved my bony wrist in front of his teeth. I held the knife clutched in my other hand, behind my back. I have to admit that once he scented mutiny he mobilized quickly and launched a preemptive strike, diving for my knees. I dodged him successfully, however, and waved the knife over my head while he bobbed about me, trying to present a moving target.

"You may have it," I shouted. "You can carve steaks out of me with it if you like. But first tell me one thing." He went on dancing like a boxer. "You made a speech last week where you said . . ."

"How would you know?"

"I have read all your speeches. I know them by heart," I confessed.

"Oh God, now you tell me. Not even my worst enemies . . ."

"In that speech you were the statesman—the statesman this, the statesman that . . ."

"I was talking of the prime minister. He likes me to call him that whenever possible."

"All the same, for God's sake hold still and listen: 'The statesman,' you said, 'feels responsible not only for the best but the worst possible outcome.' I want you to tell me in plain English for once what you mean by 'worst possible outcome.' It's an apology for the status quo, isn't it? For the war in X? I think it means that you'll do anything to stay on top of the heap."

He lunged and succeeded in knocking me to the ground.

"There's my answer," I cried. "But why are you so afraid of me, a poor shoeshine boy?"

"I'm in control," he gasped, closing his fingers on the handle of the knife I had relinquished. What he might have done next I'll never know. With the first explosion he rolled away from me and buried his head in his arms. The second explosion rattled the door in the concrete ceiling of the bunker. The third led us to believe that a ten-story building had collapsed on top of our shelter. But you know better than I do, having seen the footage I was never permitted to view, that it was only a three-story townhouse—not unlike the one several blocks away where Goethe was born—that blew up, beginning with the terrorists' cache of homemade explosives.

When the last of the rubble had fallen and the dust settled on the scattered limbs of our poor captors, the local fire department hauled us out roughly. Order was restored only with the arrival of the federal authorities. That night on television the F.M. was asked to comment on his ordeal. "Bah," he dismissed it. "To be expected. In our time assassination is the sincerest form of flattery. Tomorrow as scheduled, my visit to Dachau."

We went there in a motorcade large enough to have undertaken the invasion of an armed camp rather than a state visit to a defunct one. A dozen army helicopters droned above our cortege, barely clearing the treetops along the autobahn. As on the day he hired me, the F.M. invited me to share his armored limousine. Since the rescue he had scarcely let me out of his sight. Perhaps he was afraid I might be approached by the German scandal sheets. Or perhaps he was rewarding what he chose to consider, with magnanimous condescension, my loyalty in a pinch. The road from Munich out was lined with elm trees coming into leaf. Too soon we were at the walled compound, where the F.M. was to place a wreath on a simple plaque, laid in the ground so as not to detract from the harsh authenticity of the milieu.

If patriotism is the last resort of a scoundrel then the scoundrel's cheapest jape is to organize another ceremony to honor the harmless dead. They at any rate have earned their amnesty. To see the living tug it away from them, like a blanket too short to share, was more than I could bear.

Yet the F.M. was uncharacteristically genial, even tender, on that day, with his entourage, the press, his foreign counterparts. I heard a German official whisper something about a true statesman. I suppose he meant the F.M.'s composure after the previous day's ordeal. Not being a statesman myself I was in a nervous trance. I trembled, my mind was like running water. I shunned the patronizing glances of those around me. No doubt they thought I was there for safekeeping, on the verge of a breakdown. Whereas I was only there to visit my parents' grave for the first time.

They went to Dachau in forty-three. The records show this. How they avoided going sooner I was never able to learn. While they were in hiding, wherever they were in hiding, my grandmother lay in the damp basement of a Catholic hospital outside Berlin. She was put down in the basement because she was hopelessly senile and the sight of the two SS guards flanking her bed might have troubled the other patients. The two were waiting to arrest my parents when they showed up. The Nazis placed too great a faith in our family piety, it seems. My father left his mother behind, as I had left him earlier. One afternoon, however, my grandmother had a brief moment of lucidity. She looked around and saw the two figures standing at either side of her bed. She reached out to embrace both at once, imagining, naturally enough, that they were my mother and father. The two startled thugs leapt for their rifles but it was too late. By the time they took aim, she was already dead.

Deine Sorgen und Rothschilds Geld, my poor father used to say. I know now what he meant by that. The world is old, the standard of suffering has been set impossibly high. Who has the right anymore to complain?

There was some little trouble with the delivery of the speech the F.M. had prepared for the occasion. Someone had had the idea of giving him a megaphone so that he might make himself heard over the drone of the helicopters. But although he shouted to wake the dead, it was impossible to catch more than a few words of his speech. The sun beat on our bare heads. Two of the F.M.'s secret service people, making up for the previous day's lapse, flanked me as assiduously as the SS had my grandma's bed.

I had not expected to find, in a sort of museum at the entrance to the camp, that hideous Nazi attempt at a Dada assemblage: a great mountain of discarded shoes. No, those who wore them had been discarded. The shoes had been saved, neatly lashed in pairs. For what? If the dead could rise, that pile of shoes had a reason for being, might even be construed as an emblem of hope. If not . . . But I was unable to push this thought to its awful conclusion. At that moment a heavy hand was laid upon my shoulder. The

F.M.'s bodyguards had retreated momentarily so that he might stand beside me.

"There you have it," he said with that euphoric tenderness that had marked his speech all day. "There's your worst possible outcome. Why, it's a shoe clerk's nightmare."

I am a small man but giving him massages had put strength into my fingers. I got him by the throat with my two bare hands and held on for dear life. It took four of his men, their zeal whetted by the previous day's disgrace, to intervene. And that is how it came about that I was the last prisoner to be liberated from Dachau. If my exit in handcuffs inside a military police van bound for Munich can be called liberation. I, who ought to know better than anyone else, maintain against all the evidence that it can.

The Bus

Not only was he a self-made man, he had made himself many times over. The catalog of trades that had claimed him—none for long—ran up and down and clear through the rungs of the social ladder. He had lived the kind of life our country was once famous for letting men live: auto-didact, tinkerer, builder of fortunes from scratch. Although, to tell the truth, the only fortune he put together in all his years of roaming from the Yukon to the Rio Grande came from the till of a secondhand bookshop he opened on the main street of a small college town in the midwest. His customers were young men and women barely half his age and fresh from home. They respected him immeasurably because he had never been to school. "You ought to write a book," they said when he hinted at some episode from his teeming past. That drove him wild. Did they really think his life was over at fifty? After a few years he sold the thriving book business at a good profit and bought a Greyhound bus. He painted it bright blue.

There was room inside for a fridge, a stove, two folding beds, a whole library on tropical agriculture, and a good store of Minnesota winter wheat. Also a hammock, a tent, a collapsible canoe, enough canned food to feed a man for half a year, a snake bite kit, and thirty yards of mosquito netting. One of the things he liked about the bus was the roller over the windshield, where you could crank out any combination of letters you chose. It didn't have to spell a geographical destination; it didn't even have to make sense. It could proclaim a state of mind, a pure emblem. He chose his emblem, WILD GOOSE, and left, alone in a bus that had seated sixty, for Belize.

The last British colony in the New World had recently passed a homestead act, hoping to draw English-speaking settlers to its underpopulated swamps and forests. In Belize, in the tropics, the American dream of fifty acres and independence was still within a man's grasp. So he had read. So he believed.

He did not believe in failure. He had always found that as long as you keep an open mind and your health you can profit by your mistakes. The mistake in this case was to have chosen a climate unsuited to his health. The sun burned his fair skin, the river gave him jaundice, the muddy tracks that stood for roads tried to swallow the bus whole. Before he could clear a half-acre of mangrove swamp the winter wheat had rotted in the sack. Even the passive pleasure of bird-watching was denied him by an insidious fungus that ate the lens of his binoculars from within. The only thing that functioned beautifully during the long listless days of his recovery was the shortwave radio that brought him Texas Baptist stations and, a hair's-breadth away on the dial, Radio Havana. Like peasants all over the world, he turned to his radio for solace. Texas country western music made him homesick, but it was a woman's voice, singing the same cool songs night after night from musically conservative Havana, that spoke to him of a tropics without mosquitoes and thunderstorms, a lazy comfortable tropics that did not have to be earned by the sweat of one's brow but only received. The lesson he drew from all of this was not that he was too old to homestead in the bush, but that he probably could not do it alone any more. He needed a helpmeet.

One night in February as he lay in his hammock it began

to sway and jerk wildly, as though the two trees to which he
had tied it were playing tug of war, with him as the prize.
He fought his way clear of the netting and rolled to the
ground. The ground jumped up and tried to buck him. In
total darkness he groped toward the bus while the earth
heaved and wrestled to be rid of him. Once inside the bus
he lay down on the folding cot and fell asleep again. The
bus bobbed gently on its high wheels as though carrying
him to safety along a paved highway. When he awoke and
looked out the window next morning, he was surprised to
find himself just where he had been the night before. It was
only toward evening of the same day that he learned from
his radio of the disaster that had struck five hundred miles
west of his campsite. He got out the maps and located the
epicenter of the worst earthquake to afflict Guatemala in
two centuries. It should be said to his credit that he didn't
know the whole truth yet. It was nearly a week before the
radio gave the death toll of twenty-five thousand, and by
then his calculations were complete. When disaster strikes,
land values drop. The fainthearted move out and the stout-
hearted, with a little capital, can move in. Two months later,
when the rift in the Panamerican highway had been sealed
and the danger of typhoid was past, he set out across the
jungle to seek his fortune one more time.

The road through the Peten took him past the jungle
homesteads of peasants who unlike himself had succeeded
in clearing their half-acre for spring planting. Their
method was brutally simple. They felled the large trees—
mahogany, ceiba—with an axe and then set fire to all
the rest. The sky was full of haze. The land was black
and smoking. He judged by the scarred legs and sunken
eyes of these homesteaders, by their children in dusty shirts,
their women worn to sinew and bone, that their experiment
in tropical agriculture was scarcely happier than his own.
He had a feeling that if while driving past he'd waved
an arm out the window, Johnny Appleseed, and called
"Come on, hop aboard," they'd have abandoned their

charred fields and thrown in their lot with him, no questions asked.

He had a book in the back of the bus written in 1840 by an Englishman who had made the Grand Tour and still called Lake Atitlán in Guatemala the most beautiful place in the world. Could be. Within twenty miles of the lake he could already see, beyond the last line of wooded hills, the bluish peaks of three ancient quiescent volcanoes. He was surprised to find wheat growing at six thousand feet, gold in the golden sunlight. But the wheatfields scattered among strips of woodland were no bigger than the blanket on your bed. Pretty to look at, all that green and gold, but he didn't see a place for himself in this landscape, where the patchwork valleys and steep terraced slopes bore witness to a thousand years of steady cultivation and unsteady accommodation between crowded groups of men.

Just outside the village of Sololá, where the steep descent to the lake begins, a man stood in the path of the oncoming bus. As he rolled to a stop, Jim saw that the man wore a uniform of an indeterminate shade of green. He could have been army, police, or national guard. He didn't ask to see Jim's papers, however, but only wanted a lift down to the lake. It was a perilous descent and Jim was glad of the man's company. Three times they had to stop and back up to the very edge of the cliff in order to guide the bus into the sharp, steeply inclined curves. Halfway down Jim pulled into a lookout point with a thatched roof shelter. He didn't want to miss the famous view, the glassy lake dappled with cloud shadows, the three volcanoes rising majestically from the southern shore.

"Pretty, isn't it?" The policeman, if that's what he was, said this with offhand proprietary pride.

"Some road," Jim ventured. "Straight down the cliff."

"Going up is worse," the man said. "Who knows if your bus will make it." *Quien sabe* can be a strong negative, strongly ironical.

"Oh, this baby will go anywhere," protested Jim.

"I suppose it even floats on water," the man said drily.

"For that I have my canoe on board," Jim accepted the joke. The man grunted, unwilling to find or concede the last word.

The lakeside itself was a disappointment after the dramatic descent. The highway petered out into a row of gas stations and small shops, along a sandy track from which other sandy tracks ran at right angles down to the shore lined with ugly new hotels. Behind the narrow strip of village the cliff rose, a wall of green shot through with wavering threads of silver which were waterfalls. The village seemed to have suffered little in the recent earthquake. The church, the market, and the post office were still standing. The post office was crowded with young Americans in cut-off jeans and unfashionably long hair, mailing packages of Guatemalan homespun to friends who ran shops in Boston, Denver, and San Francisco. They reminded Jim of the kids who used to hang around the bookshop, raw boys who couldn't tell shit from Shinola. He decided to park the bus on the beach for the night and head south the next morning.

The woman on the line ahead of him in the post office was wearing a denim skirt with a large ruffle, a straw hat with a floppy brim and tall espadrilles. She was apparently buying stamps with pictures of birds on them. She paid from a coin purse she took out of a straw pocketbook she'd been carrying in a large raffia bag. The whole fussy procedure took some time. When she turned around at last, Jim's patience was rewarded with an apologetic smile.

"You're a bird fancier, eh?" he asked as she glided by him. She stopped in her tracks as if embarrassed by the attentions of a stranger, but also as if she owed it to him to listen to whatever he had to say.

"Oh, when they fly into my field of vision, I'm always delighted," she answered him. "I don't go out looking for them of course. I'm much too lazy for that." Another apologetic smile, and she was gone.

In less than half a minute he had collected his mail and was out in the bright sunlight again. He spotted her swinging her raffia bag as she headed toward the market.

"Do you live here?" he asked, catching up with her.

"I don't know," she answered. He could tell she was being scrupulously honest rather than cagey.

"I see," he said.

"I wish I did know. I'm trying very hard to make up my mind."

They had arrived at the raised concrete platform under a corrugated tin roof that housed the open air market. They climbed the steps together.

"Don't let the decision weigh on you," he said.

"Oh, I don't," she assured him quickly, as if accused of complaining out of turn. "It's the most beautiful place in the world and the people are so gentle, after Mexico. I suppose that's because it's such a small country."

He learned while she shopped for a ripe pineapple and a firm melon that she had lived near Mexico City with her second husband, a jeweler from New York. That after his death she had sold the house in Mexico and gone south.

"What do you do all day?" He couldn't help teasing her.

"Nothing much. I look around. I swim in the lake every morning. I was a librarian back in the States," she added again in some sort of self-justification no one had asked for.

His eyes lit up. His bushy eyebrows twitched.

"No kidding. I'm an old bookhog myself. Want to see my library?"

"I'd love to. I didn't know there was a library in this town."

"There wasn't till an hour ago," he boasted, glad that the night before he had changed the legend of the bus to read BOOK SCOUT. He was thinking of hunting for Spanish incunabula in Guatemala City.

She laughed so readily at the collapsible canoe, the rusted tins of cranberry sauce and chili, the mildewed collection of *National Geographic*s, that he would have been offended if he didn't know who she was. Didn't he know? He had found his helpmeet. She put a hand on his shoulder and begged his pardon.

"I'm sorry, but it's just like Robinson Crusoe, on wheels."

"I felt like Robinson Crusoe sometimes out there on the river. Whole weeks when I had no one to talk to. Not even a parrot." She ignored or failed to catch the invitation in his voice.

"Do you know," she went on brightly, "I've never seen a bus like this in town before."

"I've always been a trailblazer," he said modestly. She thought he was perfectly charming.

Back in New York after her husband's death, she had found herself living alone for the first time in her life and prey to nightly terrors. Some friends advised her to take pills. Others suggested she buy a gun. A psychologist she saw only once suggested both. He was not impressed by her analysis, after five years out of the country, of American decadence.

"They're reviving fashions I wore only twenty years ago," she told him. "What will they revive twenty years from now? The whole past is already used up. There's nothing left. And there are no children in the streets any more. Where are they?"

"Oh, I think we'll come up with something when it's time," the psychologist said. "We're a pretty resourceful bunch." A second-generation American himself, he imagined that she, the daughter of a diplomat, had had too easy a life.

"I never realized what an old country ours is," she said dreamily. When she thought of Mexico, on the other hand, she saw the view from her bedroom window: four children having their hair combed on a winter morning in the chilly stone patio of a crumbling adobe house. The house nearly a ruin but the children vivid, although they waited quietly for their turn. A woman—aunt, mother, cousin, it didn't matter—was dipping the comb into a glass of water and shaking it out. The drops glinted before they fell. Laura did not try to communicate this vision to the psychologist who probably would have said she was confusing her own fear of abandonment and death with the American destiny. But he was not a complete fool.

"You might be happier south of the border," he told her, "since you're used to that life. And your money would probably go a lot farther."

She had come to Panajachel because of the lake and because it seemed to lack the kind of entrenched expatriate colony she had known in Mexican towns, where the colonial architecture fostered a life she had come to abhor. The elegant adobe fortress, built to shelter bureaucrats of the Spanish empire, ancient redoubt, Pompeian villa, private Alhambra, its stout patio walls, overhung with bougainvillea, defining the boundaries of a wood and stone homeland, narrow substitute for the one left behind. In Panajachel she rented an ugly red brick house with a tin roof. It belonged to a doctor from Quetzaltenango and stood on a strip of land that had once been a coffee plantation. Untended rows of coffee bushes still put forth their red berries in the shade of taller trees, orange, guava, papaya, jocote. She collected the fruit as it fell and let it rot in baskets or gave it away to anyone who came to ask. It was far too much for one person.

Or even for two. The bus was parked now in the shade of the row of tall spruce at the edge of this derelict finca. The policeman had had the last word after all. The old Greyhound bought in Minnesota was not equal to the mighty ascent from Panajachel to the highway south. The sacks of winter wheat had been moved to Laura's kitchen cupboards. She rummaged in cookbooks but found no recipe calling for slightly rancid grain. The waste bothered her. Jim on the other hand had already forgotten the existence of those sacks. The fruit trees of Panajachel had caught his eye, the papaya especially, with its long gray-green bole and the cluster of round fruit ripening out of reach under an umbrella of jagged leaves. His thoughts returned to the river in the jungle, and along the river to a neat and pleasant orchard of dwarf papaya trees even the shortest worker could pick clean in no time.

He told Laura his idea. The global grain belt was shrinking fast. It would be another generation at least until tropical agriculture took up the slack. Less grain meant leaner cattle, tougher meat, and a demand for the enzyme of the papaya which is a natural meat tenderizer. Orchards blossomed from his fingers as he talked. Laura listened and grew pensive. He was a small solid man with a fine head of curly white hair. A man who had made his way in the world, at least as far as Central America. But his ambitions, so sudden, so simple and complex at once, frightened her. Wasn't she his principal ambition now? But she had already told him she didn't plan to marry a third time. Once divorced, once widowed, more would have been unseemly. She kept that word to herself however.

They might have gone their separate ways, she back to the States and a small regular dose of Valium, he on to Tierra del Fuego in a new car, if the doctor from Quetzaltenango had not reneged. He sent his agent to the house one morning. Not only his agent but also the mayor, also the head of the local tourist office. One man, three titles. Someone to be reckoned with. Not a self-made man but a man with an image of himself. It shone like a highly polished shield from the tips of his narrow shoes to his neatly knotted silk tie. The doctor's family would be spending the summer in Panajachel, he informed them, while certain repairs necessitated by the earthquake were made to the family residence in Quetzaltenango. The earthquake had provided a refuge to more than one type of scoundrel. Jim challenged the visitor. Laura was afraid of his quick temper. He hadn't yet combed his hair that morning. He was wearing a reasonably clean white shirt and his old wash pants and no shoes. In Guatemala the shoeless had better keep quiet. Laura tried to signal this to him and went to make some coffee.

When she returned to the porch Jim was showing the mayor his collection of seeds culled from papayas he had enjoyed. The mayor in his capacity as head of the local tourist bureau told them about a wonderful wild place behind Livingston, at the other end of the republic.

"No mosquitoes," he boasted. "Know why?" He paused to savor their ignorance.

"Why?" Laura obliged him.

"Because the Sweet River brings a breeze that blows them all away. The nights are delicious. Have you ever seen a manatee?" Neither of them ever had.

"You will there," he stood to leave, "hundreds of them."

"What do you say, princess?" Jim was sold. "I'll unload the bus and buy a camper tomorrow."

"Mrs. Selig will know of another house for rent near here," Laura said. She was not ready to be a homesteader's helpmeet. And who would buy, overnight, a bus that couldn't leave town?

Mrs. Selig was the widow of a German planter who had introduced a new cash crop to Guatemala. The seed of this plant was pressed for a comestible oil greatly prized in Kuwait and Saudi Arabia. Tall, ugly Mrs. Selig owned two thousand acres of choice farmland on the Pacific coast, a house by the lake in Panajachel, another in the capital, and several apartment houses in Houston. She also owned a Great Dane named Siggy, famous on the beach for his ability to retrieve a tennis ball from a hundred yards out in the lake. Mrs. Selig still had a strong throwing arm. She had sized Laura up at once as the kind of woman who needs looking after, probably by a man. She didn't know of any houses for rent, or if she did she kept it to herself, but her son had an acre with fruit trees for sale on the other side of the river, in the Indian section of town. A Dutch botanist had made some improvements to the property and then pulled out after the earthquake. There would be no extra charge for the improvements. Jim smelled a bargain.

"Let me buy it for you, princess." He struck terror in Laura's heart with such rash generosity. The one person who might have given her advice, Mrs. Selig with Siggy snuffling at her feet, could not in this case be relied upon. Laura wrote her grown daughters in the States. They wired back, "Marry him, Mom." She would not be bought. In the end she and Jim each put up half the price of the acre and the one room adobe house with improvements. The deed of sale was like a marriage contract, Jim thought, with their two names written side by side.

The Selig property lay halfway between the beach and the highway (unpaved at this point and leading only as far as the next Indian village, a mile up the lake). Sandy paths flanked by open ditches, for rainwater and sewage, wound between tall hedges of hibiscus that marked the boundaries of the native compounds. At night there was always the lulling sound of water running in the ditches. Jim's challenge now would be to make this acre into a home worthy of his woman. Eden was a slum by modern standards. He wooed his woman with mahogany planks, coiled yards of rubber hose, and the promise of electrification. He who had embarked to build a fortune in the tropics found himself hanging shelves in a hut in a sleepy resort town. She who had fled the expatriate infatuation with real estate, the continual dealing with masons, carpenters, and seamstresses, all because labor was cheap, had become the mistress of a permanent construction site.

They were bound to quarrel. Not with each other, they liked each other too well for that. A third party was needed. There was Juan, the gardener, standing motionless with one arm extended, and his hand cupped around the garden hose trained on the same patch of ground for a whole hour at a time. Laura had hired him to tend the doctor's grounds because she felt responsible for the doctor's lawns and rose bushes. He was not the best gardener in the world, she admitted, but none of the rose bushes had died.

"You could plant a forked stick in the ground and hang the hose on it for the same result at less expense," Jim pointed out.

"It's a small expense really," Laura said. She only paid poor Juan, who had four younger brothers at home, ten dollars a week. "If he weren't working for me he'd have to go down to the coast and pick cotton for Mrs. Selig and I know they need him here at home." She felt responsible for the boy of sixteen as she had felt responsible for the doctor's roses. She couldn't help it, that's the way she had been brought up, to feel responsible. Poor Juan, slight, smooth faced, always agreeable, had a way of turning his head to one side when she relayed Jim's orders, a way of hunching forward slightly to signal his ready obedience, that cut her to the quick.

"He's servile because he knows he's cheating you," Jim had said. "You have to look out for your own interests, princess. You can't always be taking the opposing side as well."

"We're not opposed that I know of," she said gently. "We quite like one another. At least I like him. Besides," she added, uncomfortably aware she was shifting the argument to a lower plane, "he's honest. That's worth a great deal in itself."

Adobe is made of mud and straw. When there is no straw, pine needles are a good substitute. One day Jim rented a truck and went with Juan up to the forests of Quiche to gather pine needles to strengthen the walls of his house. Laura was lying lazily in the hammock Jim had strung between two great mango trees, and looking up into the sea of shiny dark green leaves, when he returned. She took one look at him and knew she ought to have gone along.

"Where's Juan?" she asked without thinking, and then added, lest Jim accuse her of abetting the enemy, "Did he do his share today?"

Jim sat on a tree stump to catch his breath. "He climbed a

tree, a ponderosa, no branches till thirty feet up. In half a minute he was swaying at the top." He didn't sound angry, only perhaps envious.

"He's just a kid, after all," Laura said, and went to get Jim a glass of water and thought, as she added the purifying drop of iodine, of her own son who had dropped out of school and was selling sporting goods in Aspen.

"I take it he came down again in due time," Laura said, watching Jim drink.

"Might as well have stayed put," Jim said. "On the way back he refused to ride in the cab of the truck with me. Damned if I know why. And on that last stretch before Solola we hit something. I braked and nearly went through the windshield. Look at that." Now that the red had subsided from his face she could see the long welt. She caressed it with two fingers.

"The worst was, know what we hit?"

She shook her head. Small boys often stood at the edge of that strip of highway, dangling little ornaments their mothers had fashioned from bent wheat stalks. In their eagerness to make a sale, they ran in front of passing cars.

"The most beautiful weasel I ever saw in all my days as a trapper," Jim said. "Completely mangled."

Laura began to laugh, although it made Jim still angrier.

"If Juan had been riding shotgun I'd have known to swerve in time. Instead he was sleeping on a bed of pine needles in the back of the truck."

"He's just a kid," she said again. This time she heard herself speak and understood she was protecting a son from his father. She had divorced her first husband when her own son was only eight years old, a thin, harried little boy who took no joy in life. She had vowed then never to side with a bully again. This memory unleashed again the superstitious fear the lake till now had held in check. She was doomed to relive the past, her own shallow past, and when there was nothing more to relive, when the script was out . . . But Jim wanted her to sit on his lap. She complied with her eyes fixed, beyond him, on the dark leaves of the mango tree that completely blocked their view of the lake.

The morning after this forest expedition Jim woke and found the right side of his body slightly stiff, slightly numb. He had trouble finding some words and others he substituted in strange, poetic ways. For weeks he persisted in calling Laura Rima, as if Petrarch and W. H. Hudson and the woman he loved were scrambled in his brain. He had had a stroke.

The doctor from Quetzaltenango prescribed complete rest for six months. The pine needles had been dumped behind the hut and there they remained under a sheet of rainbow-colored plastic. There would be no more building for some time.

Laura bought Jim a new pair of binoculars to replace the ones the jungle had eaten and he took up birdwatching again. One day in August six species of hummingbird visited the garden the Dutch botanist had planted and Juan kept alive with patient watering. Laura was severe with him now, in deference to Jim. No matter how far to one side he turned his head, even if she had to address the tip of his left ear, she told him what had to be done and he did it. But in the afternoon, when Jim napped, she often let the boy leave early. It took him two hours to climb back up the mountain to his family's huts, at the edge of a cornfield enclosed with rope fences to give a handhold on the steep slope.

Mrs. Selig had been wrong. Laura did not need someone to take care of her, she needed someone to look after, to engage her inbred sense of responsibility. Caring for Jim she forgot the gloomy foreboding that had assailed her the day he killed the weasel. She made plans for the uncharted future. In a bookshop in the capital she had begun to buy children's books in Spanish, *Alicia en el País de las Maravillas*, *Cuentos de los Hermanos Grimm*. Illustrated in Czechoslovakia, printed in Barcelona or Buenos Aires, they were ridiculously expensive, but she could afford them. One day she removed her dusty espadrilles and climbed onto the driver's

seat of the bus and cranked in a new destination: BIBLI-
OTECA. When Jim was well again she would invite the
neighborhood children in and read to them, the many children she saw each day, filling enamel saucepans at the com-
munal fountain or waiting while their mothers, in long
pleated skirts of many colors, settled the tall plastic
amphorae on their stately heads. Even in Eden, one wanted
to be of use.

And for a while it was Paradise. At six each evening Jim
looked at his watch and raised a finger, lord of creation, to
summon forth the song of a whippoorwill from somewhere
among the tall trees at the edge of the Selig land. At eleven
each morning the postman blew A-440 on a pitchpipe
pressed between his lips while both hands sorted through
the mail. The days passed serenely between these two pip-
ings, one wild, one civilized, and both blessedly predictable.

Legend and Jim's old *National Geographic*s had it that the
lake was a mile deep at the center. Everyone knew the
streams that fed it but no one had ever seen the place where
it emptied out again, underground, on the southern slope.
Laura couldn't stay away from the lake. Who could resist a
pull that deep? One Saturday in December she covered her
body with expensive grease and swam out several hundred
yards from shore, beyond the dugout canoes headed for the
outer villages of Matthew, Luke, and John, beyond the cit-
ified water-skiers in their ugly rubber bodysuits. She trusted
herself in the water. It was the only place she felt safe when
alone. Not alone, after all, because the water was all around
her, a mile deep. They say whales were once terrestrial ani-
mals and returned to the water, abandoning the land, the
solid rock foundation of temples, cults, rites, castes, divi-
sions, and oppressions. The urge to build was resolved in
water. Way out where no one saw her, Laura took in a
mouthful of water and lying on her back sent it spurting
upward, as her children had loved to do in the Gulf, as
whales do in *National Geographic* photographs. Then she
turned and swam slowly back to shore, dressed, and started

home. She was fifty-five years old that week. She had to re-
strain herself from skipping like a child.

The house was dim inside at midday but the concrete
floor was cool and rough under her bare feet and her hair
dripped pleasantly. "Jim," she called, waiting like a child for
him to come take her wet things. But no one came to help
her. Jim was in the bus, listening to the rapid conversation
of a young man with the stiff bearing, the straight dark
brow and pale cheeks of a plaster saint in a Spanish church.
Laura had to listen too. They understood at once that he
was the messenger sent to deliver a truth they had perhaps
known but had not cared to examine until now.

And even now they resisted. Jim went so far as to question the accuracy of Lucas's report. Laura was bewildered
only by the tone of his narration. Was it disciplined courtesy, a natural aloofness in his nature, or a superhuman refusal to mourn that allowed this young man to bear bad
tidings so lightly? He told them he had been sent from Barcelona to continue the work of two brothers—it became
clear only a few minutes later that he meant brothers in the
Jesuit order—whose plane had crashed and burned in the
jungle two months before. The crash was an act of sabotage,
he told them offhandedly, directed against the Jesuit mission in the Peten with its orchards, library, schools, and
farmers' cooperatives.

"How dreadful," Laura said. One had to say something.

"Yes, isn't it dreadful," Lucas agreed eagerly. Laura had
never met anyone who had so completely succeeded in cast-
ing off the leaden cloak of gravity Dante assigns to hypocrites. The resulting freedom gave his speech a bare, rapid,
abstract quality. You could have called him a gossip.

"And why not?" Lucas went on. "Why not priests along
with lawyers, dentists, union leaders, and school teachers.
You know how many school teachers they killed under this
President we have now? Fifty-six so far." He clucked with
disapproval like a mildly vexed schoolteacher himself.
Then, too well bred, it appeared, to bore his hosts by harp-

ing on a subject, he picked up Jim's old guitar and tested
the strings, one by one.

His gospel, after all, was one of joy, not of horror, although from the day he came looking for the Dutch botanist and found instead this American couple, this childless
Swiss Family Robinson, they would remember him in both
horror and joy. After dinner, which he ate as avidly as he
talked, he tuned the guitar and opened on the table in front
of him a sort of pocket breviary, where in a neat archivist's
hand he had recorded all the known verses of the songs he
proceeded to sing for them with the evident self-satisfaction
of a born performer. He knew how to vary the repertoire,
alternating self-mocking Mexican ballads of unrequited love
with the plaintive chants of house slave and mine slave under the Spanish colony. Nothing human surprised him, not
greed, not cruelty, not death. Was that it? Or was it simply
that the performance counted and not the words—this moment of unquiet contentment even Jim accepted, setting
aside his autodidact's mistrust of priests and martyrs. It was
late when Lucas lifted the guitar by his neck and swung it
over his shoulder and set it behind him. The three friends
sat together on their straight-backed wooden chairs, like
travelers loath to go their separate ways.

"How will you be going down to Sayaxche?" Laura asked
at last.

"By plane from Guatemala City," Lucas said. There was
something about him that did not presage martyrdom. His
slightly fatuous enjoyment of an audience, the careful re-
cording of verses others were content to fake or forget—he
was tied by a hundred threads to a personality, a cultivated
life. Or was that what martyrdom was? A sudden brutal rip-
ping of all the threads?

It was Lucas who said what Laura was thinking. "You're
not afraid? That's good." Jim shrugged.

"What kind of foreigners are these?" Lucas asked archly.
"Living in the bushes with the Inditos, lending them money,
giving them books to read." He clucked with mock dismay.

Laura shook her head. It was true she had lent the postman's son a few books. He had brought them back the next day and asked for others with more pictures.

"It's fine," Lucas concluded gaily, standing and offering them both his hands. "I can say ex officio that you two enjoy special protection." He was careful not to add, "the protection God gives to fools and little children."

When Laura and Jim were married some time later, he said he thanked the Guatemalan government for giving him a wife. A few months after Lucas came and went, all visas were canceled and foreigners ordered to register in the capital once each month. As Laura's husband, Jim was able to spare her the monthly ordeal of a long wait in the sinister ground-floor office of Gobernación, in the same complex of buildings, it was said, that bred the lists of those priests, doctors, and teachers to be eliminated in the name of national security.

"How can you go on living in a place like this?" the young tourists would challenge, when they called on the American couple living across the river. This pair of expatriates was the closest thing to a representative of the local government that the tourists were likely to meet, and one had to make one's position known. The truth was that neither Jim nor Laura wanted to leave. Jim had made himself over again. He was in the export business now, shipping rare and minuscule orchids to the Chicago flower market once a week. The orchids grew wild in the cloud forest near the top of the volcanoes. He had only shipping costs and Juan's salary to pay. Juan, the great tree climber, was an invaluable orchid scout.

As for Laura, she was responsible now not only for Juan and his brothers, but for the postman's boy Valerio who was proving such a quick student of English, and for Hortensia who did the laundry one day a week with a baby strapped to her back and another playing at her bare soapy feet. And responsible first of all for Jim who had risked his health to build a pleasant two-room dwelling with electric light, hot

and cold running water, and who stood on line in that sinister building once a month to obtain permission to go on
living in the house he had built with his own hands.

Laura had already decided that her policy with trouble
would be as it was with birdwatching. She would not go
looking for it, but if trouble came her way, if for example
one whose name was on the lists should come to her for
help, she would do as the occasion demanded. She would
hide them on the bus. She, who had been too fearful to live
alone in New York, would somehow find the courage when
the time came.

It came quite quickly. The soldiers appeared one Saturday morning before breakfast. Two of them held their
weapons in firing position, but, on the order of a third who
was evidently their commanding officer, they let the rifle
barrels drop toward the ground. Jim recognized the officer
whose rank he could not decipher from his insignia. Nor
could he have said if the man's uniform was of the same
indeterminate shade of green as on the day he guided Jim
and the bus in the steep descent to the lake. Jim was about
to tell the man he'd been dead right about the bus, that it
was still sitting in Panajachel after all this time, but he reflected that the officer might not welcome such familiarity
in the presence of his men, although with their broad blank
faces they looked like raw recruits whose opinion no one
could value.

Laura came out of the house as the officer was telling Jim
he had orders to perform a search.

"What exactly are you looking for?" Jim asked quietly.
"Perhaps I can help you locate it," he added wryly, to show
Laura there was nothing to fear.

"Contraband," the officer replied. The word emanated
directly from Washington, from the first public utterances
of a new Secretary of State. The Secretary had since made
other statements refining and indeed contradicting his original vehement use of this word, but, as so often with words
from up north, it had taken on in Central America a life of

its own. Perhaps that was the Secretary's intention. Jim, who never read the papers, was nevertheless able to gauge the force of this word when the two recruits, having handed their rifles to the officer, began to dismantle Laura's house and garden.

"Over my dead body," he would have said to them if it hadn't been for his wife. For her sake he stepped aside and allowed the two dumb kids—they could have been Juan's younger brothers, except for their clumsy zeal—to dump the books off the shelves. They were not used to handling books and it showed. They took them by the covers and shook them roughly so that the pages flapped open. To Laura their mistreatment of the books recalled a form of torture in which the victim's arms are pinned behind his back. It was she who found the courage, although neither then nor later did it occur to her to call it that, to berate the officer in charge of the search.

From then on she and Jim were allowed to do the work themselves, bringing each book, each embroidered pillow and potted plant to the officer for his desultory inspection. The man's evident boredom Jim interpreted in a favorable light: the search was a mere formality. And so it was, because the officer had spotted the moment he arrived the thing he was sent to obtain. It was like moving day for a while, with Laura giving orders nervously to the recruits, who obeyed her like hired movers. But Jim worked hardest of all. In an hour he had unplanted every bush and tree he'd put into the Selig acre, so that the captain could glance wearily into the holes where the broken roots had networked through the soil. Laura forced back her tears for Jim's sake. She measured his distress by the fearful energy with which he flung his spade into the ground.

When it was all over, there was still the bus.

"The bus is contraband," the officer said. "You failed to report it when you got your visa last month or the month before that. The same applies to the shortwave radio. Also those." He pointed to the last two sacks of winter wheat, enough to feed a small band of guerrilleros for several weeks.

"But that bus is my home," Jim protested, too tired to use caution any longer. "It's not a vehicle, it doesn't go any more. It's like those birds, you know, the pie-billed grebes, that have lived on the lake so long they've forgotten how to fly." Banter was his only means of appeal to this cop.

It didn't work. One of the recruits—who would have thought he possessed such great mechanical skills?—was massaging the motor of the bus, and the other was pouring gasoline from a jerrican into the tank. It was he who swung into the driver's seat and started the motor running while the captain took his place beside him. The third soldier stood in the doorway of the bus with his rifle aimed at the world outside.

When the people of the village saw the bus tearing down the broad road to the dock, the soldier driving like a demon, the white-haired man running behind, they imagined there had been an accident at the lake, perhaps a drowning. If any tourists had been waiting for the ferry across to Santiago that morning, they would have seen a colorful crowd of village types gathered at the dock. And when, after half an hour of dickering with the unhappy ferry captain, the soldiers had succeeded in loading the bus onto a concrete barge hitched to the little boat, the tourists would have been amazed to hear the unmistakably derisive shout of triumph that went up from that little band of crab fishermen, fruit vendors, cooks, and waiters.

Jim in great fatigue understood what part of his life was over. The blue Greyhound was now drifting away on the blue lake, as if the color he'd chosen for it back in Minnesota had foretold this solution. For it was just that, he saw now, a solution, a joke, a revelation. There was a way out of Panajachel for his bus and it had taken the Guatemalan Ministry of the Interior to find it. It was a lesson, a sign that he was not meant to live forever on the narrow edge of a crater filled with water. He was torn between the desire to run back to Laura with his discovery and the tantalizing vision of the bus, now a small bright silhouette against the open sky, an island on the open water. And with his old eagerness there came a new ambition: on a warm sea, on a sweet river in some far part of the world, Kashmir perhaps or New Zealand, he would see what life was like on a houseboat. He had turned his back on the lake and taken the first steps into that alluring future when the unpredictable Guatemalan earth reared up and threw him to the dust. His hands grappled briefly with the ground but this time it tricked him by lying perfectly still to receive the entire weight of his body.

His vision was incomplete. The bus was not drifting freely, it was being hauled at great risk by a small rundown ferry not made for such heavy work. A woman Laura would have recognized because she sold green onions at the Monday market in Solola was kneeling on the lower deck. She did not kneel to pray but because that was her normal posture in repose. There were two worn circles at the front of her long dark skirt, from much kneeling. As the noon wind came up from the south, however, and beat the gray water against the sides of the boat, she shut her eyes and said a brief prayer. For who could say if the monstrous large bus thrust upon the water against all custom and good sense would not founder, dragging the ferry and all its passengers to their deaths in the treacherous lake.

The Autograph

Once at a party his wife introduced him to a movie star, the only movie star they'd ever met, saying "And this is my husband Michael, the quasi-sabra." The movie star looked at the small plump man with the broad face and sandy-colored hair and thought, he doesn't look like a sabra and he certainly doesn't look crazy. Then someone else came up to meet the celebrity and he forgot the mad Israeli altogether.

In the seventh month of his sabbatical year from the college where he taught accounting, Michael Czerny decided to go to Europe. His wife was all in favor. So were his mother-in-law, sisters-in-law, and children. It had made them nervous to think he was wasting a year of God-given free time smoking too many cigarettes and producing nothing as he paced his little office on the second floor of the family house in New Jersey. The office, which would have made a very nice guest bedroom, had been set aside for him when the family moved from the East Village, where Michael had written his first novel, published some ten years before.

On the back flap of the dust jacket Michael had permitted his publisher, an independent house in those days, to run a brief biography. "The author left his native Berlin for Israel when he was only five years old. He fought in this war for independence and came to the U.S. in 1953. He has held a variety of jobs including barber and peach-packer in California. He has just learned to drive." (The impending move to the suburbs forced him to that.)

What he did not permit the publisher to do was to append a photo of the author, wings of his shirt collar pressed flat over the lapels of his one good jacket, flyaway sandy hair pressed down for the cameras. He was against publicity except as regarded his work, which received the following mention in the Sunday *Times:* "The author's nameless, faceless hero lives through a number of Excedrin headaches that do not seem to touch him any more than they did this reviewer." Michael's clever sister-in-law had written an irate letter to the editors citing Marcuse and Max Brod, in his defense. Michael was touched by this display of erudition and family feeling but nevertheless, since learning to drive, he had not written another word.

Why not? The family wondered and worried. As he had never obtained any sort of university degree, publication of original works was the only path to promotion open to him at his college. And although they had secretly laughed at the first novel—it read like a translation from Turkish, why didn't he write in his native German or Hebrew? Did he think he was Conrad or Kafka?—they were also secretly impressed that someone had seen fit to publish it at all, even accepting Michael's many strictures: no author's party, no press interviews, and that silly pseudonym, Schwartz instead of Czerny. Now what kind of false modesty was that?

Besides, they reasoned, the publisher knew best. If he thought Michael had talent, who was Michael to shrug and say, whenever questioned, "Why should I write another book? There are enough books in the world already. Too many in fact. Besides, we already have one author in the family."

He meant his wife, Carol, who had lately begun to publish small books for small children. These had proved immensely popular with teachers and librarians throughout the country, and even children seemed to enjoy them, to judge by the quantity of letters they wrote Carol. Many of these letters she had framed under glass and they now hung in her office (formerly the sun porch) which was larger than Michael's and given character by a large collection of antique dolls.

"At least he's not jealous of my career," Carol told her mother one day. "Some men would be."

"Of course he's jealous. Why do you think he stopped writing?"

"I liked what he said about Stendhal the other day," the gentle soul demurred.

"Sour grapes," Michael's mother-in-law ruled. For Michael had another line to silence inquiries into his literary progress.

"If I could write like Stendahl, then I would owe it to humanity. As it is . . ." A shrug of his shoulders completed his meaning.

Now his mother-in-law was uncharitable and therefore wrong. Michael passionately admired Stendhal, who like himself had been plump, unprepossessing, and yet successful with women. *Amour de tête* or *amour de coeur*, this passion had been with him since first reading *The Red and the Black* in Hebrew at the age of fifteen. It was in imitation of the master's famous dry style that he had striven to banish clutter, including names and faces, from his own work. It was following the master's system, the silence and cunning of Beylism, that he had chosen to publish under a pseudonym. In fact, the whole purpose of his intended trip to Europe—that journey the family hoped would bring fresh inspiration to their flagging author—was to permit him to acquire an autograph or letter from the hand of Stendhal or Beyle or César Bombet or the Baron de Cultendre. The great man had penned a hundred volumes under as many false names. Surely in the whole of Europe there would be some scrap of paper bearing his signature that Michael could possess for less than the six hundred pounds he'd recently seen quoted in a Sotheby's catalog.

Shortly before his departure he took his wife into his confidence.

"Pussy," he began in his unabashedly philosophic mode, "as you know, I am a modest man. I have no material ambitions. There is however one material possession I covet in all the world, and this is it."

His wife understood and approved. She imagined he wanted the autograph as a talisman or amulet to guard his creative powers, in which she had never ceased to have faith. Besides, she was something of a collector herself. The daughter of poor immigrants, she understood that tradition must be built from scratch out of trivia. What counts is not content but fidelity to form. Thus she was proud, for example, that her best friends were women she had known in grade school. And thus each morning she admonished her children to drink their juice before it lost the vitamins. She wasn't really worried about the vitamins or their loss, but that was what her mother had said to her each morning at breakfast. Most mornings before school the child Carol had been too agitated to drink anything at all, but the words were precious to her—even if they still gave her a slight tremor in her stomach—because she had heard them once and could repeat them now.

Of course she had been raised in a dingy apartment in the Bronx and her own children were growing up in a three-story house in New Jersey, with attic and basement. This did not represent a break with tradition but rather provided tradition more scope. Attics and basements were where one traditionally stored the early mementos one's children would someday cherish as relics. The autograph, she thought fondly, would be one of the relics.

Michael was careful to cover his traces by telling the rest of the family only that he was going to Frankfurt to see his friend Goldkind receive an award from the German government as the most valuable Jew left in Europe. Michael was being facetious. Actually he believed that even if guilt alone had prompted the Germans to come across with the prize of twenty thousand marks, his friend Goldkind's books had richly earned the sum. And he was looking forward to seeing Goldkind for the first time in five years. They had met when both were down and out in New York in the late fifties. Goldkind worked in a barbershop near Union Square and tried to place Michael there. But whether Michael's hand actually trembled on the razor, as a customer alleged, or whether it was only his sly, provocative style of conversation that put the customers out, he was fired within a week. Shortly thereafter he had met Carol and moved in with her on East Tenth Street. Her salary kept them both for two years while he wrote his novel without sequel.

She drove her husband to the airport one evening late in March. Sitting in the lounge waiting for his flight to be announced, she did not resist an impulse to slick down his hair and straighten his collar.

"What brand will you smoke over there?" she asked as Michael broke a Camel in two and stuck half in his pocket for later. She wanted to suggest that he cut not only his cigarettes but his smoking in half but she didn't like to sound bossy.

"I'll buy a carton or two of Camels on the plane. And a bottle of brandy for Goldkind."

"Poor guy. Give him my love, won't you."

"Why poor? He's getting twenty thousand marks tomorrow. I should be so poor."

"It's not as though it will make him happy for long," Carol said. Hadn't Michael told her a dozen times in the past week, in a tone that others might have thought was begging for contradiction, that Goldkind lived like a real artist, in a rented room in some hag's apartment, no furniture, few clothes, scarcely any friends of either sex. He lived, Michael had said over and over as though nagging at a bad tooth, for his art.

"Maybe you can get him to buy a new suit," Carol said. She knew Goldkind well from their days in the East Village when he had dropped in almost every night at dinner time. "Oh, and I have a going-away present for you." She looked at her husband lovingly. He was the source, the dusty pollen and scant nectar of her happiness, even if it took a steady effort on her part to turn these into a small uniform supply of honey. She handed him a notebook small enough to slip into a jacket pocket and compact enough to hold a month's worth of pithy observations. It was a brown notebook, the color stationers call manila. When she was a schoolgirl all her notebooks had had covers of that nice honest brown.

She was not altogether sorry to see her husband go. His idleness had turned him cantankerous of late. He stood in the doorway of the children's rooms and wanted to chat while they were doing homework or fiddling with the computer. He prowled in their rooms while they were at school and poked among their belongings. No, she was glad he was going. The trip could only do him good. But the notebook was more than a subterfuge to start him writing again. She hoped that in some way it would later permit her to share the voyage with him.

Michael found Goldkind in a deep depression. He had just finished writing his acceptance speech and he hated every word of it.

"You know why I'm getting this prize, don't you? I sent you a clipping." Michael said it hadn't arrived. They were in Goldkind's room in the hag's apartment. It was 8:00 A.M. Frankfurt time, 2:00 A.M. New York time. They drank the gift brandy and smoked Michael's cigarettes.

"I had a reading in Munich this winter that was broken up by the neo-Nazi party. It was the week after they ran my face in *Der Spiegel*."

"I was always against personal publicity for artists," Michael said.

"They threw what appeared to be bags of yellow ink. At least that's what the police report said. And when the award was announced a month later some left-wing faction accused me of having engineered the attack to sway the judges."

"You never thought of refusing their lousy money?" Michael asked. When the two of them had met in New York in the fifties they recognized their affinity by the fact that both had refused any form of compensation, the money that makes it good, *Wiedergutmachungsgeld,* from the German government. In Goldkind's case the refusal was absolute: he had no surviving relations. Michael at that time still had his mother and an unmarried aunt in Tel Aviv who were getting money from the Germans and living in carefully managed self-deprivation in order to leave him the legacy they felt he had coming to him. Even after he all but broke with them and left the country, they went on stinting themselves. Carol had corresponded faithfully with Michael's mother and when the old woman died there had been a fat check for him, equivalent to the price of the thousands of jars of Matjes herring she had denied herself for his sake.

"I'm not Jean Paul Sartre and this isn't the Nobel prize," Goldkind muttered. "I need their lousy money. Besides, Sartre didn't have to live in Sweden. I live here, I can't afford to seem like too much of a snob. Bad enough I write better German than any of the pure ones, you follow?"

"Carol wants you to buy yourself a new suit," Michael said.

"She sent a check?" Goldkind asked and then added at once, "Sorry, that was uncalled for. I can't afford a new suit. The prize money has to last me five years. Five years. Nowadays who dares spend that long on a single work of art. They're all afraid of being forgotten in the interim."

"What about Grass?" Michael asked. "His last one ran three thousand pages."

"All cribbed from some medieval cookbook," Goldkind sneered, and launched a long tirade against the local competition. Michael stopped listening. His friend had offered neither food nor drink, except for the brandy, nor even a chair to sit on. And he hadn't asked after Carol either, or the children who had changed so much in the five years since Goldkind last dropped by to dinner.

That afternoon the prize-winning author strode to the podium in the salon of the Goethe House, while Michael shifted his bulk on a small gilt chair in the first row of the audience. Goldkind took his speech from his pocket and let it drift to the floor. He gripped the lectern with both hands and began, extempore, "How odd of god to choose the Jews. This sentiment, so compactly formulated by a minor Victorian poet across the channel, is surely yours today, when our esteemed jury members play the role of god and I alone am called to represent the remnant, etc. etc."

Goldkind had refused the *geld* of his native land but he was not above cashing in on a little guilt, etymologically akin and morally worse, in Michael's view. The gilt chairs creaked and groaned under the weight of Goldkind's captive audience, tortured by the spectacle of his own self-torture. Who was executioner here and who victim? That's what comes of having your picture in the papers, Michael thought sadly. Still, Goldkind was a great writer. Allowances must be made. His *Cutthroats Barbershop* was a work of genius.

Three days later Michael left for Paris. He found the city not improved and immensely more expensive than when he had passed through on his way to the States. After paying twelve dollars for an *assiette crudités* at the Brasserie Lipp, he made his way to the Bibliothèque Nationale where he managed to ascertain without benefit of French that, under a new policy of regional decentralization, the entire Stendhal archive had been transferred to Grenoble, where it could perhaps be seen at the Musée Stendhal. Michael was neither a pedant nor a sentimentalist. He had no particular desire to walk the streets Stendhal had walked or to lay red poppies on his grave in the Montmartre cemetery. He had only one thought in mind: the autograph. Therefore he took the

next train to Grenoble and registered at the Hotel de Sa-
voie. Having asked for a room with a view of the Alps, he
was shown to a freshly carpeted broom closet overlooking a
dank courtyard. Never mind, he didn't plan to be spending
much time indoors. When the museum opened the next
morning, he had been waiting on the steps for half an hour.

*From the Files of the Commissariat de Police, Centre Ville, Ville de
Grenoble, Departement de l'Isère, 5 avril 19—*

At five o'clock on the afternoon of April 5, 19—, an American citizen by name of Michael Czerny was arrested as he was
about to exit from the Musée Stendhal, place Grenette. He
was taken, under police escort to the municipal jail, where he
was booked and detained on charges of theft with intent to
defraud the national patrimony of the French people. The accused made no attempt to deny the charges against him, not
only because he is totally afrancophone, but because he had
been apprehended in flagrante. There having been found in
his possession a small brown notebook (Exhibit A) concealing a
letter (Exhibit B) with the following text:

*Je soussigné Pierre Daru, Intendant Général de la Grande Armée
Impériale, vous prie d'accorder toutes les facilités au porteur de cette
lettre, Monsieur Henri de Beyle, dans l'exercice de ses fonctions comme
etc. etc.*

Attempts to ascertain just how the letter was removed from
the locked display case labeled "Stendhal in Moscow," were
postponed pending the engagement of an interpreter. The accused, as mentioned above, speaks no French. Nor, despite the
possession of a valid American passport, does he appear to understand English. In fact he has walled himself, since the moment of his arrest, in an obstinate mutism that has occasioned
his confinement in an isolation cell on the top floor of the municipal jail.

It was only in court during the fifteen minutes it took to
decide his case, that Michael learned that the purloined letter did not in fact contain a Stendhal autograph, but was
only a note of introduction penned on Stendhal's behalf by

a high official of the Napoleonic quartermaster corps. Hearing this, Michael imagined the judge would drop the charges against him. But the good bourgeois of Grenoble did not fail him, any more than the court of Besançon disappointed the expectations of Julien Sorel. When the judge, who seemed a decent enough fellow, sighed and said, "Ten thousand francs or thirty days," Michael held out his empty hands. The evening before his trial he had been permitted to make one phone call. Of course he had phoned Goldkind in Frankfurt and told him he might need to borrow a large sum of money for a few days. It was hard to hear his friend's voice because of a shrill yapping noise in the background. Had it not been for the noise, however, Michael would have had to doubt Goldkind's word when he told him he had invested the entire award money in a poodle coiffure salon he expected would bring in a steady but modest, he repeated modest, income for the rest of his days.

"Paris is damned expensive, I warned you," Goldkind said. Yap, yap.

"But so beautiful at this time of year," Michael replied, glad to hear that his true whereabouts were unknown to the world. After that he could face his trial and sentencing with a light heart.

You will say, "Ah, but you've skipped a scene. No fair. Why did this law-abiding family man, whom you have led us to believe was perhaps quasi, but not crazy, suddenly commit a theft in broad daylight and in a foreign country to boot? What was his motive? Where is the searching analysis of his emotions to which we readers are entitled as readers? Was it stupidity, cupidity, a gratuitous act? Or only the weather?"

To which I reply, Ah, but what possessed Julien Sorel to shoot his beloved Mme de Renal during Sunday Mass at her hometown church? The scholars are still arguing that one in the *Cahiers Stendhal*. The question is a favorite at thesis examinations wherever French is spoken and in several places where it is not.

Michael, be it said to his credit, scorned such questions. His own novel, *The Obsession,* although conceived as a footnote to *The Red and the Black,* (something not even his wife or his editor would learn), deliberately ignores it. His slight work begins at the moment Stendhal's masterpiece is over: with a sudden, seemingly unaccountable murder. For Michael the motive is unimportant. The consequences are all that count.

What if—he speculated—Julien Sorel, having shot and wounded Mme de Renal, and being ready to accept his punishment, were instead reprieved, not only pardoned but lionized, made a celebrity, a laughingstock, robbed in short of every last scrap of that privacy (born of others' incomprehension) that gives *The Red and the Black* its sublime coda. This is the fate to which Michael subjects his own nameless hero, the victim of a series of absurd coincidences too complex (and perhaps too boring) to relate here. All the poor fellow wants is to be put to death in peace. Instead he lives and loses his mind.

It was Stendhal who settled that silly dispute between the classicists and the romanticists by pointing out that today's classics are the romances of an earlier era. He would have smiled on Michael's clumsy attempt to update the story of Julien Sorel, the hero who chose death over a career under the Bourbon restoration, thereby exercising a negative sort of freedom. Now Michael too knew something about negative freedoms. He had been raised in Tel Aviv among survivors of the death camps. The ladies his mother had to tea wore long sleeves on the hottest days. Their euphemism for dead was "shipped out."

When, as a very young man in Tel Aviv, Michael came across this line in *The Red and the Black,* "In our time we commit acts of great cruelty without being in the least cruel ourselves," he knew he was the reader for whom Stendhal had written, the generation of 1930. Unhappy member of the happy few, henceforth he was burdened with a sort of moral and intellectual *noblesse oblige.* Just as Stendhal had subverted the fairy tale in which the peasant triumphs and marries the princess, so Michael, proceeding with the times, took it on himself to measure the distance between Stendhal's fairy tale—Julien's redeeming stay in solitary, his lonely ascension to the scaffold, his severed head borne off on a platter—and the great leveling operations of our century so prodigal of mass graves.

Once he had carried out this obligation, it seemed to him he had nothing more to write. Who would be a bearer of bad tidings? When, his first book behind him, he began to say, "If I could write like Stendhal," he was not being merely coy. He was wishing the times were different. For only in Stendhal's day had it been possible to write, with whatever prescience, like Stendhal. In the late twentieth century it was possible only to write like Michael Czerny/Schwartz.

He had grown up keenly aware of negative freedoms: freedom from starvation, from freezing to death, from lining up to be shot or gassed. After that whatever else came was pleasant and easy and why complain? A modesty so ingrained that it seemed to have determined his slight build and pale coloring also shaped most of his public and private behavior, his contented drudgery as a tenured lecturer in Beginning Math. ("Tenure is a form of slavery that dates from the late Roman Empire," he liked to say. "Mortgages are a later refinement.") The rest of his character—whatever ambition or deep discontent he knew—he summed up, self-mockingly and with some vanity, in his expressed desire to own a Stendhal autograph. The autograph was the object about which a fluid inner life had crystallized, to use the Beylian term. No wonder then that after several days of familiar intercourse with the desired object he surprised even himself by daring to take possession with a fine disregard for all the rules of society and his own nature.

Michael, of course, would never have given as many pages to his motives as I have. He might be flattered by so much attention, but it would also make him uneasy. "I'm really much less complicated than you make me out to be," I can hear him say, putting on his modesty like a mask. False modesty, therefore, and bound to evoke the disapproval of his entourage. But that was precisely its function. Their disapproval released him from further unwanted scrutiny, just as the judge's verdict of guilty was to release him, for an entire month, from the world and its obligations.

No, he did not dwell on his crime, but only on its consequences, which were wholly unexpected and wholly to his liking. For one thing, he found that the rest of his vacation abroad would not cost him a cent. Goldkind would have been envious to learn that his friend was now an official guest, all expenses paid, of the French Republic. What's more, Michael would not be obliged to wear himself out seeing museums and other points of interest that were of no interest to him. He was free to pace his cell, meditate, revolve his thoughts, and smoke *Gitanes tabac blond*.

His life in the sequestered cell on the top floor of the Grenoble jail was regulated and free from material preoccupations. It resembled the regime at one of those austere writers' colonies in New England where your meals are left outside your door on a tray. Except that in jail the tray was delivered through a slot in the door of the cell. The metal grille that covered the narrow window did not spoil an excellent view of the *Aiguille du Midi*, still clad in snow at its peak. Such mountains Michael had beheld till now only on the wrappers of chocolate bars or on calendars. Now his window was his calendar. Each day he watched the sun rise and set through another of the thirty small squares of the grid imposed on his view of the Alps. When he had watched for the thirtieth time, his vacation would be over. But he was in no hurry.

No beautiful jailer's daughter fell in love with him and braved discovery to visit him in his cell. Although naturally enough in the circumstances he dreamed now and then about something of the sort, he hardly expected life to imitate art with such pedantic precision. And if she had come, that Clélia or Louise of his dreams, she would have been a distraction. For on his third day in captivity, he had begun to write. In short order he had used up whatever paper he could find in the cell and had made notes on his cuffs, his wrists, and the inside of his prison canvas shoes, until he got up the courage to ask the guard who brought his meals for writing materials. As the guard was a former *pied noir* of Corsican origin, they were able to converse in rudimentary Arabic. Afraid of running out of paper again, Michael devised a system of abbreviations and acronyms to which his native Hebrew, for this time he wrote in Hebrew, lent itself very well.

It may have been the lack of exercise coupled with excessive mental stimulation, or it may have been the cheap red wine served with his midday meal, but one afternoon, waking from a nap, he looked at the window of the cell and beheld a series of parallel ladders reaching to heaven. The rungs of the ladders were girt with fire. He leaned over, found his glasses under the cot, but by the time he had them on and had wheeled on his knees to study the vision, the window was only a window again and the barred sky drained of color. He smoked a *Gitane,* and set to work again, slowly, deliberately now. He had plenty of time. After all he was not writing for his contemporaries but for readers a hundred years hence. Watch for his book, if it appears in your lifetime. You will know it by the author's name, an assumed name, neither Czerny nor Schwartz, and by the missing photograph on the back of the book jacket. If it bores you, if its tone of exalted rage seems to you to be that of a pseudo-prophet, never mind. Tell yourself it was only the wine.

Stendhal completed the *Charterhouse of Parma* in seven weeks. At the end of his month in the Grenoble jail, Michael left for home, taking with him an envelope full of odd scraps of paper marked with Hebrew words and letters, and a sense of trepidation about the future. Or perhaps he was only feeling what all prisoners feel on their release into the world.

He flew home from Paris the next day. He embraced his

wife and children, first the girl, who had his eyes, and then the boy, who had his mother's. Then he sat down to dinner with his family and told them what he had seen in the Frankfurt Zoo, in the Louvre, the Tuileries. He described Chartres and several castles along the Loire, particularly beautiful in springtime. He gave them the gifts he had purchased at the airport and a stack of postcards he had not had time, on his crowded itinerary, to send off.

Long after the children were asleep, he followed his wife upstairs to bed. At the top of the stairs she paused and turned to ask, "You didn't get it then, did you?"

"No," he admitted. But he added, "Possession is nothing, enjoyment is everything." This epigram had sometimes consoled Stendhal when a mistress proved unfaithful.

"Well, now you can enjoy it all the time," Carol said, and flung open the door of Michael's office. On the wall over his desk hung a dark frame. The light from the hallway shone on the glass so that he couldn't see at first what lay beneath it.

"Don did it, you know Don, who works at the library. He's a calligrapher," Carol said eagerly as Michael, who had learned no French in his month abroad, squinted and read aloud the framed inscription: "*A mon ami, avec gratitude, Stendhal.*"

"It's a forgery," he said fiercely. "What do I want with a forgery?"

He had thought when he left Grenoble that he no longer desired the autograph. He had had the enjoyment, after all. What did possession matter? But now this fake on the wall rekindled a violent desire to have the real thing. And why? Because he was no longer the man he had been in Grenoble. He required the autograph as a souvenir of that month already lost to him that could be remembered only with impotent nostalgia, by its relics.

There were tears in Carol's blue eyes. He took her in his arms to console her. Over her shoulder he noticed that someone had laid a fresh pad of lined paper on his desk. The pale blue lines were marching across the page in pairs, like so many ladders without rungs.

Soldier's Rest

In the only country in Central America not overrun by soldiers, a tomb stood ready to receive my Uncle Arthur's remains. His enterprising wife had it built when the new cemetery opened and lots were being offered at introductory bargain rates. It was a fairly large affair. Beneath the two family names (hers, locally prominent, took precedence) there was room for Uncle Arthur to have engraved over the door Voltaire's boast *"Ma Vie Est un Combat."* Uncle Arthur chose this epitaph, he later told me, to introduce an ecumenical or cosmopolitan note, after his usually docile wife, without telling him, had arranged for a marble angel three feet tall to be installed atop their common grave. A freethinker himself, Uncle Arthur did not like the idea of being laid to rest beneath an angel's wings.

Once the tomb went up, he grew restless. He always had to take account, of course, of the ever-present possibility that the armies overrunning the countries to the north would one day converge on his retreat and string him, the first handy American, from the nearest lamppost. This eventuality did not trouble him unduly, however. Abroad from the age of twenty, he had lived and worked in every country in the free world and in border areas—Vienna, Mozambique, Hong Kong—where he represented or bent the law as it pleased his employers. Uncle Arthur was fairly certain he would see the armies converging in time to pack his wardrobe of twenty suits, twenty pairs of shoes, and fifty shirts into steamer trunks, along with his autographed photos of Nehru, Adenauer, and deGasperi, and his library in five languages. For an American, Uncle Arthur was quite a polyglot.

What Uncle Arthur did worry about, in the letters that reached my mailbox within three days of having been written in the hasty scrawl of a bureaucrat who has always relied on secretaries to decipher and polish his message, was closet space. The question was, once he got away in time, where did he hang his twenty suits and his fifty shirts to keep them from wrinkling, and if they did get wrinkled, whom could he hire to iron them for him? His wife's servants, understandably, were not likely to emigrate with him. His wife was a woman of great character and devotion and would, if required, iron his shirts herself, although to do so would not be consonant with the image of her role that she was given as a child (at a time when Uncle Arthur was already bending the law in occupied Vienna). There was nothing Blanca Lilia would not do for her American husband, but she had sworn that when the time came she would defend to the death the family estate (twenty-five acres, diminished by the greed of cousins and the carelessness of siblings) rather than surrender it to the converging armies of the north. Envisioning with perfect equanimity her last stand at the gates of the finca, she went out and bought the tomb. The price was good and the location desirable, in a freshly landscaped park halfway between home and the country club where she drove her husband each day after siesta for an afternoon round of mah jong or canasta.

Of course she did not expect him to share her Latin martyrdom. On that point she was quite emphatic, he told me later. Came the revolution, he'd be a free man.

"What do saucepans cost in America these days?" my expatriate uncle wrote. "What do you spend a week on vegetables? Can you find me a job at say $25 thou a year teaching a couple of history courses at your local university? I'd need a maid of course to prepare my dinner and supper. The supper could be light, a cold plate, if needed. How does the current crop of American girls feel with regard to older men?" The letters arrived daily, their onionskin envelopes marked, from force of habit, VIA MAR, as if we were still in the days of gunboat postal service. Sometimes there were also postcards with surprising faces—the Hoover Dam or the Illinois State Capitol. Reading between the lines of this paper blitz (no mean task, the way Uncle Arthur could cram his margins full of afterthoughts and subqueries) I disengaged his message. In all this frenetic planning for the revolution I read a gnawing fear that it might never take place. The soldiers massed at the border of his adopted country would continue endlessly to respect the lines of demarcation drawn with mere ink on mere paper. Life would go on as in the past, with daily naps and visits to the country club and instead of leaving home with his wife's blessing and twenty suits in a trunk, Uncle Arthur, dressed for the last time in the gray pinstripe that was his wife's favorite from the day they met ten years before at an Embassy party, would himself be entrunked and delivered, like a clearcut message, into the tomb with the dwarf angel whose wings already stretched and beckoned.

Before retirement Uncle Arthur was an expert organizer of tedious international conferences where the fate of the third world hung in the balance and was left, like food on the plate of a finicky eater, untouched. At the start of his career, as I well knew, he had been a joyful inventor of dirty tricks, a rigger of elections, suborner of cops and magazine editors. The more respectable he became with time, the more he liked to boast of shady exploits that enjoyed, by the time I was old enough to hear of them, the statute of limitations or the blanket pardon of the term "Cold War skulduggery."

If a revolution were needed to free him from an onerous

marriage, he would know better than anyone how to foment one. Central America would be child's play after Central Europe. When he appeared on my doorstep one evening without warning, I was sure the worst had been accomplished and that we would all read about it in the next day's papers.

For a man who had just plunged five countries into war, he seemed indecently calm.

"Glad to see me? Now you won't have to answer my boring letters," he said. A small vain man, capable of self-deprecation whether or not it was sincere.

"Where's your luggage?" I asked. He had only a flight bag. Highly suspicious.

"What do you have to drink? There's plenty of time to talk," he said, removing the silk muffler from around his neck and hanging it carefully over the back of the chair where he then draped his black gabardine raincoat. He set his small black fedora on the table next to my writing things. I fixed him a drink. He returned from the bathroom and settled onto the sofa, slipping off his shoes.

"It's a funny thing," he began after downing his Cuba Libre in two gulps. This was the line he used to introduce his troubles or anyone else's. He gossiped randomly, be it said to his credit. If he played for sympathy, it was universal sympathy. "It's a funny thing," he repeated, which is what gossips say when they want to sound like philosophers. "Stone does not erase easily. Hmm." He laughed curtly. This time the tone of self-deprecation seemed authentically bitter. "It'll cost her a fortune." He looked at me. "You don't know what I'm talking about." This in a tone of irritated condescension that his secretaries must have heard often. "The tomb, dear girl, the tomb my late wife . . ."

"Blanca Lilia is dead?" A consummation I had not envisaged.

"No, why, what did I say? A Freudian slip, we all make them. Not late, but latent. You still don't follow. Blanca Lilia and I are through. It's time to put thy pale lost lilies out of mind. My trunks are packed and sitting down there on the dock. They should be loaded on board"—he consulted his watch—"within the hour. I'm out of her life, or will be once she has the façade redone. Can't you just hear them sand-blasting my name off the tomb? What a racket, enough to wake the dead. That reminds me by the way of a story they were telling in Cairo when King Farouk . . ."

"You left her," I accused him. "There's been an invasion from the north."

"Oh, that, don't believe everything you read in the papers. Politics had nothing to do with this. My wife asked me to leave. I'm a gentleman, as you know. I gave her her will. You remember?" When I was little Uncle Arthur used to read to me from the legends of King Arthur. At six I imagined they were somehow the same person. Of course I remembered the riddle, "What does a woman want? Her will."

"Funny thing, the guy's name is actually Guillermo, William, the cousin usurper. He was in Uruguay all these years buying old cars and shipping them home to sell, making traffic jams with Hispano-Suizas on all our back roads. When the military stepped down in Uruguay he lost his business contacts, at least temporarily."

"How old a man?" It slipped out. I would have called it back if I could. How unfairly I had judged my uncle.

He eyed me severely. "You're not as dumb as I thought, or else, being a woman, you know women." He made it a term of opprobrium; this was the other face of his chivalry. "That's right, younger than I, lots younger. He and Blanca Lilia shared the same wet nurse as babies. Who could compete with a memory like that? It's a funny thing though, I thought I was doing okay. I made love to her twice a week, which wasn't so bad considering my age and a survey they just ran in the local paper down there, that had the country club buzzing. It seems their national average for married couples, they only asked women, thinking they'd be less likely to lie about getting laid—that phrase is all right as it stands unless you misplace the comma—is only 1.7 times per week. Can you believe it? I was actually .3 ahead of the national average in a Latin country. Of course on days I played tennis I didn't make love, enough is enough, and vice versa. Uruguay gets democracy and I get the boot. There's no justice."

"I'm so sorry, Uncle Arthur. It must have been a terrible shock." Or was that what he'd seen coming when he started the direct-mail campaign all directed at me?

"Well, I'm trying to be broad-minded. It's a curious thing however. When I met my wife she was just over the death of her old man, whom she had nursed for five years. She had to wipe him fore and aft and spoonfeed him his gruel. Grim. You know in these Latin families they've always given one of the offspring the privilege of devoting her prime years to the parents' declining ones. Blanca was the chosen one. If I hadn't come along when I did, who knows what would have become of her. None of the family saw her as anything but a nursemaid. I got her back into circulation. And let's face it, with all the women I've abandoned in my lifetime, it was bound to happen to me sooner or later. But so much later, damned inconvenient! I may have to buy a toupee. What do you know about this new laser treatment for baldness? Never mind, I'll ask around. My trunks should arrive within a month. How long can you put me up? Or should I say put up with me? I figure a month should be just enough to let me get my bearings. What I'll need is either a rich widow or an adjunct professorship or . . ."

"And your pension?" What was the point of thirty years in the foreign service, if not the pension?

"I got a lump-sum payment. Unorthodox, I know, but so were the circumstances of my departure from the service. You could call it severance pay."

"And what happened to it?"

"It was not all that much to begin with. Enough to build a guest house and swimming pool at the finca. Funny, when you disapprove of something you look just like your

mother. Same scowl. I still have my social security. I'll have
to get the bank down there to forward my checks and write
Washington. . . . I won't impose for long. Four weeks and
I'll be flying."

Master though he was of the *fait accompli*, Uncle Arthur
never was able to retrieve his steamer trunks once they'd
been shipped, in error, to Tierra del Fuego. He took the
loss well.

"Reminds me of a friend in Venice, a painter who had a
fire in his studio. Wiped him out completely. It's a funny
thing, you'd think in Venice the fire department would be
fairly efficient with all that water around, but by the time
they had it flowing in the right direction, he'd lost his life's
work. I sat with him that night and you know what he said?
'What a relief—for years I've been wanting to go abstract.
Now there's nothing to stop me.' Well, I don't know where
my luggage went but I surmise there are going to be some
very snappy dressers among the penguins." Small and
portly as he was, with dainty feet and shortish arms, the
quip took courage.

Rich widows were not forthcoming, however, and the
dean of the local college was being forced into retirement at
an age somewhat inferior to Uncle Arthur's.

"That's all right," he said when we sized up his prospects
at the end of four weeks, and found them not very bright.
"I'm working on Plan B. By the way, what's for dinner?"

Although it was against my principles, I made his bed
each morning before I left for work. Poor Uncle Arthur was
born in an era when unisex was rare as unicorns. Each evening I cooked for him. His favorite meal was plain boiled
rice, a taste acquired during his long postings in the tropics.
While he ate I listened to him talk himself into and out of
recurrent bouts of melancholy.

"It's a shame about the epitaph," he said one night during
the third month of his stay. "I thought that was such a dashing statement I picked out. Voltaire among the angels. Lis-

ten, if it comes to that, have me cremated and scatter the ashes."

"So that you rise like a phoenix, in ten places at once," I said to cheer him. But that night he was beyond cheering. As much as I questioned him about Vienna in forty-six he had nothing new to tell me (or old, for Uncle Arthur never minded repeating a good story).

A few nights later he brought to the table a cardboard box eight by eleven and two inches deep, and set it at my place.

"For me?" I asked naïvely, thinking my hospitality was to be rewarded.

"For posterity," he said, letting the word ring out like the last line of the national anthem. "Of course I consider you my ideal reader. No, I take that back. My ideal reader would be someone who had no idea what I look like. Lawrence of Arabia was a small man too, by the way. They had to waive the height restriction to let him into the RAF. Yes, I was surprised too when I heard about it." He gossiped about historical figures as though they were his contemporaries. To him, no doubt, they were.

"I liked what you said the other night about the phoenix. How else can a man hope to achieve immortality and ubiquity, if not through art?"

"Hitler found other ways," I said. After listening to Uncle Arthur for three months, I was not eager to read him as well.

He chose to misunderstand. "You're right. *Mein Kampf* is not all that well written and yet it's still a best seller or at least it's still backlisted as far as I know." Then I understood that not only had Uncle Arthur been writing a book in my house, he had researched the pubishing industry and mastered its jargon as if it were another small country ripe for covert action.

"How quickly can you get through it? Finish it tonight and I'll give you top billing in the dedication. And as I realize that's a dubious incentive, think of this, my dear: the sooner I sell this baby, the sooner I can afford to move out."

Next morning after three hours sleep I rose and found Uncle Arthur brewing coffee for the first time in his life.

He greeted me expectantly. "Well? How did it go? Of course I realize spy novels aren't everyone's thing. Men tend to like them more than women do." I sat down in my bathrobe. I sipped my coffee judiciously. I said in an offhand way, "Stendhal of course never gave all his sterling qualities to any one character. He gave his good looks to Fabrice, his wit to Mosca, and his soul to the duchess of San Severina."

"Yes, yes." Uncle Arthur waved impatiently, shooing a gadfly. "I probably overdid it with my hero, you mean? All right, but it's too late now, I can't write in any new characters after five hundred pages. The plot by the way is watertight. See, that just shows my intuition was right. It has to be read by someone who's never met me. If you had cooked Stendhal's dinner every night for months, and by the way, I'm told he was very unprepossessing physically, you'd find Fabrice hard to swallow."

I swallowed hard. For the first time I pitied Blanca Lilia and envied her too. She neither spoke nor understood English.

"But I'd like to enjoy what you write," I said quietly. "And you're right. Seeing less of you would probably help to that end." I put down my cup, went back to bed, and slept all day.

When I got up he was gone. His shaving things were gone from the bathroom, his bathrobe from the closet—the penguins had his suits—and his paperback copy of Bartlett's *Quotations* was missing from the shelf in the living room, along with several of my books, I noticed. There was a note on the kitchen table, under my cold cup of coffee.

It was written on a sheet of the familiar puckered translucent airmail paper. I had to turn it all four ways to follow my uncle's agglutinative sentences to their reluctant ends.

Dear Barbara,

If you weren't my sister's only daughter, I'd have made you a proposition or maybe even a proposal long before this. Don't be sore with me because I didn't. (Although I have no doubt you would also have been sore with me if I did, being a woman and thus a paradox even to yourself.) I'm leaving as much for your sake as for mine. You need to meet younger men and I need to find a publisher (or maybe publishers, depending on arrangements for paperback, serial rights, etc.—not to mention foreign editions).

Thank you for your hospitality. Expect a check from me soon, as soon as I exchange words for cash (although probably not at the exalted rate of $100 per word I was once paid by an Israeli banker I provided with a slogan for his full-page ads in the Cairo *Times*—post Camp David of course). The slogan by the way was only one word long, so he could afford to be "generous."

In case you're looking for it, I took your copy of *Charterhouse*. There may be something in what you say about my book. You have a fine mind and your boiled rice is superb. I have enjoyed both immensely. More soon.

Your loving uncle,
Arthur

P.S. EUREKA! I just thought of the only possible title for my opus: Voltaire's own "Life is Strife." Now I have to find out from Blanca Lilia if she cleaned it off the tomb, as it could be embarrassing (in case of interview by *People* magazine reporter, for example, apart from pre- or post-publication publicity) to have it in both places, book jacket and stone suit, at once. My guess is she did.

P.P.S. If the book were published posthumously (an eventuality I hope to forestall by living a good while longer d.v.) it would probably be all right to make such a double usage of the Voltaire tag. In fact in that case it might even be touching and help boost sales. What do you think?

Since he left that note, Uncle Arthur has settled in Miami and written two more unpublished novels so that, as regards his last question, it's hard for me to say, even now, what I think. What I hope, however, is that one of those aggrieved groups of plotting exiles Miami's full of has put my uncle on its bloated payroll, imagining he'll bring them luck.

In Fiona's Country

I was hungry the whole time I was in Fiona's country. It's the altitude, they told me. It's the vegetables, they're fresh year round, we have no winter to speak of. Or, knowingly, "I see you like our cooking." I began to be ashamed of my insatiable appetite. The day of the party, for example, I was eating even during the televised interview Fiona's parents had arranged for me in the museum at the front of their house, where my pictures were being exhibited.

"What do you like best about our country?" they asked as the camera focused on my mouth wide open to admit another of the fat hors d'oeuvres prepared in the long tiled kitchen by six pairs of small deft hands. I felt like the emperor Montezuma, who had to choose each night among two hundred kinds of bitter or sweet chocolate to drink, and, like the emperor Montezuma, I was full of foreboding and thoughts of cosmic mortality. Maybe that's why I kept stuffing myself with *mixtas*, *pedregales*, *flautas*, *malinches*, the whole menu. Fiona's house was not only a museum, it was a banquet hall. Everything was done there on a grand prerevolutionary scale.

"Apres moi le déluge," I said to Fiona's mother that morning when I came upon her scolding two servant girls who had flooded the veranda with an inch of soapy water. Barefoot and with their long narrow skirts—the kind all native

women wore before the war—tucked up, they were chasing the flood with straw brooms. You could see how rich it made them feel to squander all that nice clean water on a blue and white tile floor. Water was wealth, God's gift, the whole growing season in one bucket. I was sorry to see Fiona's mother chase them away, and to mollify her I quoted the king of France, Louis the something, but my accent isn't too good and she, who studied painting in her youth at the Académie Julian, did not seem to get the joke.

To be sure she had a lot on her mind just then with sixty guests coming to see her prospective son-in-law's first one-man exhibition in or out (in this case out) of his native country. Her cousin the Minister of the Interior was going to give me a plaque and her uncle who ran the TV station was bringing a film crew and a godparent at the only daily paper that had not been banned or bombed was sending his art critic who happened, as luck would have it, to be Fiona's own father.

Of course I had read—who hasn't—all those dull statistics about the fourteen families, the oligarchy who own ninety-five percent of the land and eighty-five percent of the wealth, or was it vice versa? But I didn't realize, until Fiona brought me home to announce our engagement, how convenient this made things like launching an artist's reputation. With only fourteen families to consider (and two of those had emigrated by the time I arrived) the competition was negligible. And the times being what they were, the families supported one another in every way possible. I was an outsider and thus suspect at first, but once they saw I wasn't going to make any snide remarks or ask embarrassing questions (What have you done with Dr. Milmoss?) and that all I cared for was Fiona and my painting and the *mixtas* and the *flautas,* they opened their arms to me and I was invited out every day and every day I ate well. Perhaps it was the altitude.

Fiona herself was surprised by my gluttony. She knew that back in Wisconsin I had worked my way through school clearing trays in the college cafeteria and couldn't stand the sight of food even outside of work hours. With typical delicacy she had offered to help with my tuition out of her monthly allowance—it would scarcely have made a dent—but I couldn't accept that and what would she have thought of me if I had? In her parents' house of course it was a different story. Her German grandmother quoted some proverb to the effect that the worthless guest is honored most (if I understood correctly), at which I smiled and acquiesced because I could see it would not help to say no. They would only think I was trying to ape their own exquisite politeness.

This same politeness has led the family to offer to sit for their portraits. Even Fiona's father, a busy man with a private army of three thousand to keep in line, had offered to sit for half an hour each day. I told him straight off I could only do landscapes. Trees, sunsets, hills are my forte and their country was so rich in fine views. He looked disappointed at this but I knew from experience that any portrait I did would be sure to disappoint more. Likenesses are a touchy business and likenesses of prospective in-laws more so. Yet he seemed dead set on it. We wrangled politely for a week and during all that time I didn't paint a stroke. I was just about to give in when Fiona's father took me aside one evening and apologized for his seeming insistence.

"Sunsets are out just now," he said glumly, "because of the curfew." Now to refuse anything to a guest goes against the most deeply held codes of Fiona's country. The man looked miserable. To cheer him I said at once. "Oh, my favorite hour is after three when the shadows begin to lengthen and the colors are still alive."

"All right then," he sighed. "Every afternoon from three till six you'll go out. My chauffeur will drive you to some lovely spots on my aunt's walled estate a few miles from here. At six each evening he'll bring you home." He hesitated, prey to some painful thought. "You may have to sit on the floor of the car during the return trip."

"There's nothing I'd like better," I hastened to assure him. "So good for the back." Neither of us alluded to the reason for this precaution. For him to impose his troubles on a guest was unthinkable. For me to offend my host by alluding to a slight disorder in the social fabric—the raging civil war—would have been ungrateful.

"You're sure you wouldn't rather paint a still life? Mangoes, zapotes, guavas. We could set you up admirably right here in the house. No, never mind, I can see your heart is set on the outdoors. Ah, what it is to be an artist. When will you be ready for a show? One month? Two? Just let us know."

It took me only six weeks to complete enough canvases. Each afternoon a chauffeur in the employ of Fiona's father drove me to a hill outside the capital. Doubling as bodyguard, he waited behind a tree while I worked, for you couldn't be too careful, Fiona's father said, with a talent like mine, heh heh. There was not a great deal for the man to do, except one day when a peasant, with an axe over one shoulder and a cord of wood piled on the back of his wife, stopped to watch me work. He planted himself close behind my back to observe me using tools unfamiliar to him. The bodyguard held his fire long enough for the little man to ask, "What's that for?" He pointed with a callused finger at the canvas where I had caught a good likeness of the afternoon shadows along the sides of some splendid *madrón* trees.

"It's to hang on a wall and cover the cracks," I said in Fiona's native language which was neither mine nor the peasant's.

"Ah, very good." He drawled his vowels with maddening length, a sign of respect in his circles I believe. I saw the glint of sun on steel twenty yards away.

I shouted in Fiona's language, "No go away, pig, and let me work." The peasant ducked his head into his shoulders and trotted off down the path with his donkey wife behind him. The bullet struck a rock five feet from me and glanced off.

"I need a beer, quick," I told the guard when he came out of hiding. "And while you're at it how about a couple of chicken sandwiches? Help yourself too."

He fetched the hamper from the car and for the next

twenty minutes we ate without a word. As Fiona's German grandma likes to say, Hunger is the best of cooks.

When we had eaten our fill the guard asked, "What did the pig want?" In Fiona's country the word for native and for pig are one and the same.

"He asked what this is," I said, pointing to the canvas which as it happened was my best yet.

"Mmmh," the guard grunted as if to imply the answer was too obvious to require articulation. "It's that clump of trees over there, right?" he then asked, pleased with himself for having made the identification when by rights he should have been pleased with me for making it possible. I had made great strides in the course of a month in Fiona's country. My show was sure to be a great success.

Because of the curfew the guests had been invited for an unusual hour, two in the afternoon. In evening dress of course. The occasion required it, the code was strict and, as Fiona's German grandmother liked to say, In times of need the sausage goes down without bread. She lent me her son's tuxedo and Fiona's father's valet took it in for me. Even with all I was eating I was no match for Fiona's corpulent uncles. Fiona herself came to tie my white tie. She was flushed and excited and beautiful in the gown she had worn as Desdemona in the college drama society production in her junior year. Her mother had ordered the gown in Paris and brought it up for opening night. Was Fiona a good actress? I'm no judge. She carried herself regally. She was the only girl on campus who had ever had occasion to say offstage, "Fetch me my shawl," to hired help and this worked to her advantage in the Elizabethan setting. In the great chain of being she knew her place, somewhere near the pinnacle. Back home her cousin the drama critic wrote a glowing yet intelligently qualified review of her performance and even put in a good word for the sets, which I had done. It was after Fiona showed me the clipping that I asked her on our first date. We drove her Porsche to the top of a hill behind campus and parked facing the sunset that marked the dawning of our love. I had just switched my major to art.

And here we were about to announce our engagement.

"I'm so proud of you darling, but do hold still," Fiona fussed with my tie. I had discovered a handful of stale peanuts in the pocket of the uncle's tuxedo and couldn't resist them. Why were there peanuts in a tuxedo pocket? Was my bulimia a local affliction? The peanuts in Fiona's country, I should explain, are nothing like the plebeian goobers we buy in cans and plastic bags. They are small and round and delicate and savory, handpicked and handroasted. In Fiona's country there was never a shortage of hands. The life was in all ways caressing.

"I can't wait for curfew," I murmured into Fiona's neck between mouthfuls. At eight promptly the rest of the family withdrew to their rooms and bolted the doors. Fiona and I had the house to ourselves. A little unacknowledged fear is a fine aphrodisiac. All night long I shielded my love from the foggy dews of her murderous mountainous country.

"The Foreign Secretary is coming," Fiona said. "I know it means something although Daddy wouldn't say what. Oh darling, I'm so proud for you." I spat discreetly into my handkerchief. A rotten peanut had unaccountably got into the bunch.

The first guest to arrive was the national poet, a man in his eighties with curly gray hair and long expressive fingers. He came striding across the patio waving a rolled-up parchment. He stopped just short of my nose. He bowed with amazing suppleness for a man of his years and opened the scroll with a flourish. It was a sonnet, I counted the lines. But what did it say?

"Youth inspires age," the poet said to me as if to deflect, from excessive modesty, the compliment I was bound to pay him. Words failed me but Fiona stepped into the breach.

"Oh grandpapa, how perfectly lovely." She threw her arms around the old man's neck.

"I'm deeply honored, sir," I said to the old fellow when

he had succeeded in disengaging his mobile fingers from the straps of my fiancée's gown.

"It will run on page one of tomorrow's paper," he said and added waggishly, "With the censorship you know, they're always short of copy at the last moment." That was the poet using his poetic license. For who but a poet in his dotage would have alluded to such things in polite company?

Then the rest of the guests arrived in an armored convoy and the house musicians struck up the sweetly stuttering gourd xylophone, men servants in embroidered waist-length jackets and white trousers glided about in bare feet, offering trays of goodies prepared by the kitchen divinities. On the flat roof of the one-story mansion built foursquare around an open patio, four sentries were posted belly down, one at each corner of the house. Like all members of the army of Fiona's country below the rank of colonel, they wore the uniform of the insurrectionists, just as the insurrectionists wore the uniform of the government forces. Since the social code of Fiona's country permits men to do a great many things it at the same time forbids them to take credit for doing, civil war would have been impossible without these disguises.

Imagine a family gathering of someone else's family. You are the only one there without a blood relation in the crowd. Blood is thicker than water, so much thicker in fact that I felt I was about to be ingested, as if by some giant corpuscle that would easily dissolve me and turn me into more of itself. Could that be why I had been eating so furiously since I arrived in Fiona's country? To build up strength for a contest in which my survival was at stake? Feast before famine: where had I dredged up that primitive wisdom? I was about to reach for a plump golden banana no longer than your little finger when Fiona's father came and embraced me and steered me to a corner of the veranda where he presented me to a man in the uniform of the army high command. I knew at once this must be the

Foreign Secretary from whom Fiona hoped for great things for us both.

"How do you like our little country?" he asked genially when Fiona's father had withdrawn.

"I've never eaten so well in my life," I said from the heart.

"Spoken like a true artist," he said. "The pleasures of the senses. Well, in that case, you will enjoy Paris."

"Paris?" I was puzzled and made no attempt to hide it.

"How's your French?" he asked.

"Apres moi le déluge." I tried it on him. It didn't fit.

"Well, our Fifi can give you lessons. I've just signed the papers naming her cultural attaché in Paris for the next three years. She'll have an office at the embassy, chauffeur, bodyguard. . . ."

"Bodyguard? Paris?" I had a sudden craving for bananas. Would Fiona love me in Paris as she had in Wisconsin? With all the fuss about my exhibition, no one had said a word about a wedding date. Where did I fit into this new plan?

"I've never been to Paris," I said to gain time.

"It shows," the Foreign Secretary said.

"I had thought we would settle here," I went on. I had thought nothing of the sort but it couldn't hurt, could it, to pay a compliment to the country whose uniform the man wore.

"Are you crazy?" He looked at me strangely. "I sent my daughters abroad years ago. One is with the BBC in London and the other is with the FAO in Rome. You don't suppose Fiona's father wants the apple of his eye to languish under a bushel?" He looked at me as if I were the bushel.

"But I love this country," I protested. "And I love Fiona."

"You use words too lightly," the Secretary said severely. "If you love something you must be willing to die for it. No, that's the least. You must be willing to kill for it. What have you ever loved so much that you would be willing to kill, in order to make it yours?"

"Roast suckling pig," I said with no hesitation. "Of course I'd just as soon not have to slit the porker's throat myself but I am neither squeamish nor sentimental where a good meal is at stake." I thought I had him there but before I could be sure the first pomegranate hit the patio floor, spattering red juice and slimy buckshot all about the clean tile. The Secretary threw himself under the nearest bench. The ladies shrieked, the obscene fruit rained down from all four corners of the roof, and I ran to find Fiona.

Desdemona's breast was stained with red as if she had been knifed not strangled. I swept her into my arms, past the scrambling crowd and into the museum. The paintings were unharmed, thank goodness. So were the hors d'oeuvres. By the time I had polished off my third *mixta* it was quiet again outside. I stuck my head out the door. The beautifully laid tables were a shambles. Broken glass littered the floor and a bucket had landed on the bronze head of the conquering hero in the patio fountain that now ran pale red. The first to emerge from hiding was the national poet. I joined him by the fountain. The vandals had fled the flat roof, leaving a mass of banana peels and melting ice.

"They won't run it on the first page now," the poet said sadly. "They probably won't run it at all." I nodded. The symbolism of pomegranates was not lost on me. Tables and floor were covered with seed. It looked as though a horde of small rodents had passed by, leaving their droppings everywhere.

The guests hung about the veranda, clinging to one another, waiting for the servants to come with mops and brooms to restore order. Where were the servants? I thought perhaps they had withdrawn for safety to their huts at the back of the garden but why had they not returned by now? The code forbade the other guests from acknowledging the mess but I thought I might take the initiative, being a foreigner. Gently I removed the bucket from the head of the conquering hero and wiped his bloodied face with my handkerchief. I was about to attempt a restoration of the grand centerpiece of tropical fruit—tropical fruit is notoriously squishy—when Fiona's father came running up and begged me to desist. There were tears in his eyes and in his emotion he grabbed my hands and kissed them. They tasted faintly of papaya.

"My dear son-in-law," he began. It was the first time he had ever called me that. My heart soared. "What can I say?" He would have fallen to his knees before me but I caught him under the arms so that his bent legs dangled above the ground that was littered, remember, with broken glass. I stood him gently back on his feet.

He gave a little shudder and said, "And now, my son, I must ask you to leave. Go and pack your bags at once."

"Pack my bags?"

"Why yes, we cannot offer you the hospitality of which you are worthy and therefore we have no choice but to let you go."

I protested, as surely I was meant to. It was all a game of courtesy. But no, he was firm, adamant and even, when I had protested for the third time, harsh.

"You heard what I said. You've got to go."

"But Fiona, our trip to Paris, the wedding, my television interview. I haven't seen it run yet."

"There is time for everything. Fiona and her mother and I will join you in Paris next month if God wills it. But now you will do me the kindness to leave my house this night. I am no longer fit to be your host."

I looked at Fiona, expecting her to object at last but she merely nodded at me from behind her father's shoulder. The nod meant, Yes, he's serious, it can't be helped. I noticed then for the first time how wan she looked, how hollow of cheek, how positively undernourished.

"What about my paintings?" I asked. I hadn't even had time to make slides to show the New York dealers on my return from my successful debut abroad.

"They will be shipped. Every last one. The servants will . . ."

"The servants," I cut him short. "Where are the servants?"

Fiona's father looked as if he had been slapped. He turned dead white, then spun about on his heel and strode off. His boots crunched on the shards of broken glass, grinding them to a fine powder.

"One man's distress is another man's joy," Fiona's German grandma piped up. "Were that not the case, there would be no servant problem."

"And no revolutions." The national poet winked at me and stalked off on his long thin legs. He came to my room as I was packing, oh blessed poetic license, bearing a tray heaped with all the good things we were to have had for dinner. Oh turkey seethed in chocolate sauce, oh soup of cucumber, raisins, and banana chunks floating in the broth of grainfed chickens. Oh mango and egg yolk whipped to a froth with rum. We ate togther, painter and poet, dipping and licking our fingers. We were down to the last bit of mango puree, each too polite to take it from the other, when Fiona's cousins came for me. The armored convoy was leaving and I would have to go with it. I hoped till the very end that Fiona would insist on going with me. I'm still not clear why she didn't.

"Here, these are for you." She put a silk purse into my hands at the last minute. I opened it on the plane and found it contained the petits fours that were to have been our dessert. Dear Fiona, I thought, how well she had come to know me, and I, her country.

And yet a whole month went by before I heard from her. She wrote that her cousin the drama critic had been named French correspondent by his paper. He would be leaving for Paris when she did. They had been married at home in a quiet ceremony. She was sure that as a fellow artist I would understand. I did not understand in the least. For a long time I couldn't eat a thing. The cook at the restaurant where I wait on tables is kind and tries to tempt me with a new dessert each day. But I can't forget the food in Fiona's country. It had a desperate savor to it I know I'll never find anywhere again.

Carmela

June, 198——.

Carmela can never remember which wine to serve with the tuna fish sandwiches. Both tuna fish and wine are alien to her of course. I understand this and am patient therefore. Besides, I find that such minor discomforts and disparities as my staff occasion break the monotony of an otherwise exceedingly well-ordered life. Well-ordered no doubt thanks to their ministrations but chiefly to my own signal perspicacity in hiring them, refugees from places where—if they only knew it and perhaps they do, I haven't asked them—human decencies like loyalty, service, and pride of accomplishment are still far more firmly rooted than among us.

A paradox here: Carmela fled her country to find a better life in ours, bringing with her virtues that flourish only in the absence of what she came to seek—a living wage, a roof over her head. There is a lesson in all this for the developing nations that I shall merely hint at because I surmise there is slight chance, if any, of its being heeded in our time. It has to do of course with the uses of adversity not to say injustice. The trick—for the rulers of the emerging nations—would be to maintain injustice at a level that molds character without souring it. Once this level, this *mediocritas aurea,* has been passed in either direction, there is always the devil to pay as the course of events in our country from 1932 to 1980 clearly illustrates.

To return to Carmela, however. This otherwise perfectly charming and devoted person has very short legs, nature eschewing the liberal fallacy that holds perfect equality among all members of the species to be possible or even desirable. Carmela on the other hand is eminently desirable and the fact that she has to take three steps running for one of mine has served to establish our relationship on a footing altogether appropriate to our respective sex and station.

A man lying under a hedge looks less tall than he does standing alongside it. *Hic jacet lepus* as my old classics master at St. Paul's used to say while forging *ex nihilo* as it were the Latinate style that gives my readers such comfort they tell me. Carmela asked me under the hedge to obtain a visa for her brother who had been turned down by our consul in Tegucigalpa. The protocol of these sessions of ours (although strictly speaking neither of us was seated for any length of time: I fell on her, she went down like a wisp of hay) required that she arise and depart while I, out of respect for her Latin modesty, feigned slumber on a bed of twigs and ant nests.

When she committed this first breach I simply ignored it. Her English was of such tentative and doubtful cast that I could with no trouble at all pretend I hadn't understood a word she said. I knew that once she returned to the house and her ironing she would bethink herself and be glad to let things go on as they had during her two years with us. In all that time there had been no mention of a brother, indeed no mention of anything extraneous to her duties as a member of my household staff which at the time, under the Caribbean Basin Initiative, numbered seven.

Once while waiting to board a plane in Louisville I made a mental calculation of the amount I saved each month by having Carmela iron my shirts instead of sending them out. The sum was a considerable one and as I boarded the plane

I had to congratulate myself on a well-run domestic economy and on my undiminished capacity for quick mental arithmetic. My mother informs me that by the age of five I had committed the entire times table to memory and it is as fresh in my mind today as when I first mastered it. In the course of a state banquet last month at which I happened, unaccountably or in consideration of our long friendship, to have been seated at the President's right hand, I found myself telling him about this little talent of mine. He whose hearing is no longer as sharp as his practice imagined I had said "timetables" and astounded his postprandial audience by reeling off the entire schedule of afternoon flights from San Diego to Los Angeles. "Correct me if I'm wrong," he said concluding this spellbinding recitation on a characteristic note of modesty. Needless to say none of those present either could or would. Correct him, that is.

At home however the following day I did check on the timetables I keep in the bottom left-hand drawer of my desk and found he had misspoken himself with regard to the 11:45 flight to L.A. I felt I ought to call this to his attention, lest the lapse be used against him later on by some ungracious adversary. *Humanum errare est* began memorably the wire I got off at once. Only too true, alas. Western Union is no longer capable, it seems, of transmitting figures accurately, and I'm afraid that although the intention was honorable the result was nil.

August.

For the past few weeks although I've seen Carmela coming and going I have avoided giving pursuit. Was it my imagination, or had she, lacking the exercise of the chase, begun to put on weight? Ever in favor of on-site verification, I returned to the fray. She was as usual compliant and conducted herself with that discretion I have learned to prize in her no less than her small firm breasts. But when she left the bathhouse where my yacht winters in drydock, I noticed that a letter had been left lying on the weathered planks. This startled me. I had not known that Carmela could read or write.

Literacy, I have long since concluded, is a great handicap in women and indeed in most men. Universal education gave us Marx, Hitler, and the Ayatollah Khomeini. Those who regularly deplore the high dropout rate at our inner-city high schools are either fools or hypocrites or, as I have long suspected in the case of my good friend A. M. Rosenthal of the *Times,* both. Imagine all the young muggers at large in our major cities united under a single banner, fired by the subversive twaddle of some half-learned pamphleteer and you will understand the mischievous error, now happily being rectified, of federal subsidies to public schools and public libraries.

The letter was from Carmela's brother. If I would procure him a green card, he said, he would take a job as a dishwasher in far-off California, where Carmela would be welcome to join him. When she brought my lunch tray I confronted her with the missive and saw at once by her helpless smile that she had not a clue as to the contents, had merely transmitted it, like the dutiful creature she was.

I was so pleased to find her after all as innocent of letters as her Creator made her, that throwing caution to the winds I offered her a bite of my sandwich. (Bologna on rye, it being Thursday, with a dry Riesling.) Embarrassed by this sudden kindness, Carmela blushed and murmured, "May God repay you for this kindness."

"Not God, my child, but you yourself shall repay me at the earliest opportunity," I told her. She left in a delicious state of confusion.

After lunch I went to the library and spent a pleasant hour copying out the family tree in the paternal line, beginning with my great-grandfather James P., who fled Ireland with only the shirt on his back, at the time of the potato famine. I sent this off to Tegucigalpa with a bit of kindly advice. There are after all by any reckoning several million illegal aliens in our country who have not only managed to cross the border undetected but who continue to evade the INS while they take advantage of those same opportunities that lured to these shores my ancestor, whose grave in the potter's field at Doylestown I make it a point to visit once each decade.

I suggested to Jose that if he lacked the gumption to enter the country on the sly, he probably wouldn't make a go of it here anyway, and might as well stay put where he was. And as for the green card, I thought, tossing the letter into my mahogany out box, Carmela managed perfectly well without one.

December.

My wife and I long ago invented a little game of forfeits that we continue to play with undiminished pleasure after thirty years of marriage. Each time her picture runs in *Women's Wear Daily* she puts five dollars into the kitty and each time mine runs in *Time* or *Newsweek* I forfeit the same amount. Thus do we make instant reparation for that state of humility the Evangelist enjoins on us, and at the end of the year we find we generally have amassed sufficient to throw a great bash, to which we invite, *par un juste retour des choses,* the offending editors of the offending publications.

On the day of this year's festivities my wife burst into my bedroom without knocking and flung at me the silken garment she had been planning to wear. It was arguably ruined. When I had succeeded in calming her somewhat, she revealed the source of the damage. One of the housemaids had fainted while standing at the ironing board. My wife had come upon our Haitian cook slapping the poor girls' face, to revive her, and had been told, by the cook, that Carmela was probably suffering the ravages of a parasite endemic to her filthy country. My wife was sure the cook was right. Carmela's stomach, she informed me, was visibly bloated while her face was thin and drawn. She didn't suppose I'd have noticed. I said of course I hadn't. My wife had placed the girl in quarantine and was distressed to think she had been allowed to help prepare the feast for our guests.

The notion of communicating a tapeworm to much of the New York press corps was one that promised a certain poetic justice. I knew however that the chances were slight. "I doubt very much whether the girl's condition is contagious," I attempted to soothe my poor wife, who left to dress, leaving me to repair to my study to complete a speech I was to deliver the next day at a meeting of the OAS in Washington. My subject, as usual: overpopulation and underdevelopment.

A man in my position requires very few ideas and after a certain age, no new ideas at all. No one has read the books that I have read. I find that most audiences, moreover, have very short memories, and that speeches I first gave in 1956 are quite acceptable in 1986 provided only that certain references, viz. the name of the president in office, the parties to wars being waged, are scrupulously updated. This is a chore I generally leave to one of my secretaries who are all blood relations and thus perfectly trustworthy, but at times I take a certain perhaps perverse pleasure in imposing the task on myself. This night was one of those times.

Filling in the blanks was an occupation well designed to soothe my shattered nerves and suppress unwanted thoughts of what the morrow might bring. My wife had made an appointment for Carmela with old Dr. Jacobsen for ten o'clock. By ten o'clock next morning with the grace of God I would be airborne and in fact, if the plane ran to schedule, would be passing twenty thousand feet above the spot where my great-grandfather James, peace to his bones, lay in the potter's field at Doylestown. Adjusting my black tie for the evening's entertainment it occurred to me in a fleeting moment of such lassitude as Pascal would well have understood, to envy the old man's estate.

Once aloft next morning and on my way to address an audience whose applause was assured me by the nature of the occasion and my own gifts, I saw things in a rosier light.

As I shook hands with each of the delegates from the Caribbean Basin I found myself speculating about the child Carmela would bear me. Would he be short and dark and curly-haired like the delegate from Colombia, or would he be long and thin with high cheekbones like the representative from Guatemala? I am opposed on principle to too much mixing of the blood, not on biological grounds—although I suspect they also exist—but for solid historical reasons. The founding fathers created a political system in keeping with their education and temperament. What that system might become in the hands of people whose essence differed radically from theirs, I do not hope to live to see.

Not entirely lacking a sense of humor, I found it quaint that I should have contributed all unwitting (the procreative act is always in some sense unwitting) to the bastardization of the race. This led me while half listening to the modest proposals of the delegate from Chile, to consider the vagaries of fate, the accidents of birth, the sallies of destiny that make us what we are. Raised under my roof, Carmela's son (I have begotten only sons) would take his place among the nation's elite. Raised elsewhere . . . well, as his mother would have said with a sigh of resignation, *Pues, quién sabe.*

At last it was my turn to speak. Addressing the assembled delegates of the lands to the south I felt suddenly that I was addressing my own people. It is not easy to fool one's kin. I couldn't help but notice for once that my speech fell flat.

"The south doesn't count," my friend Henry K. admonished the new Chilean ambassador not long after the election of the ill-starred Allende. I had not ceased to share this view and yet the merely polite applause of those representatives from around the equator cut me to the quick. It was not vanity. I know vanity in all its vain manifestations. No, something creaked and groaned and gave way inside me and I recognized by its passage a true feeling: one of keen disappointment. It was as if my own son, the one about to be born, had grown to manhood and turned away from me.

By the time I left the lectern I knew what course I must

take. The child would be raised in my house, would learn to walk on the lawns I paid three gardeners to tend, would learn to sail the sloop that had taken me twice across the Atlantic, learn as I had to write Latin hexameters, row with the first crew, and take whatever degree young men of his generation were taking in order to prepare themselves for a life of public service and public acclaim.

Now I do possess considerable powers of persuasion as a public speaker and in the give and take of debate I always shine. What would I say to my wife when I got home? How induce her to move Carmela out of the servants' quarters and into the second guest bedroom? A preliminary confession was in order perhaps before moving the question of moving Carmela. Words seldom fail me nor did they now. As the limousine sped northward that night along the Merritt Parkway, my pen made rapid progress across the page.

Errare humanum est. The chief and grievous error of liberalism has always been in failing to recognize irreducible human weakness. The basis of my conservative creed, on the other hand, is a conviction that evil exists and that all the constraints evolved during milennia are scarcely capable of holding human nature in check. From this general premise, which my wife shared or she would not be my wife, I intended to move cautiously toward the specific and anecdotal substance of my plea. Here my pen faltered until as we entered the long gravel drive leading to the big house, I steeled myself for a feat of extempore delivery.

To deliver several speeches in a single day would not have fazed me once, but now it was beyond my means. I admit that when, half an hour after my return home, it was made known to me that at some time during the course of the noisy party the night before Carmela had quietly packed her scant belongings and vanished, I felt only relief.

It was not till next morning as I sat staring through the window of my study at the empty lawn running down to the empty beach, the tall hedgerows along the path, that the child returned to my thoughts. And since that day he has never left them. In vain I wait for a letter from the semi-literate brother, a postcard, a plea, a threat. Nothing comes. The other night at dinner I sat across from an old colleague at the CIA. There is nothing this man would not do for me if I asked it, and little at all he could not do if he would. And yet I held my tongue.

The child is mine all the same. I measure my remaining years by his. I see him twenty years hence, pushing my wheelchair across the lawn. I see him—this is far more likely—clad in dappled green, in the depths of the green jungle, leading the fight against everything I stand for. My son, wherever he is, will be a leader of men. I feel quite sure of this. He will not be lost among those yearning masses to the south. You will see his picture in the papers often, and fear him when I am gone.

Hortensia

The stewardess on the Swissair flight from Geneva to Mexico City was not aware, when she seated the two middle-aged women in well-cut suits and short fur jackets at the same table in the first class lounge, that she had committed a great gaffe. Mrs. Allende recognized Mrs. Kirkpatrick at once. Mrs. Kirkpatrick did not appear to recognize Mrs. Allende, who opened the conversation with a remark about the weather. Chileans are as adept as the English at this kind of innocuous patter. The stewardess served a bottle of white wine, and from the weather the two women soon progressed to more intimate topics. Mrs. Allende, at the proper moment, informed Mrs. Kirkpatrick that she was a widow and Mrs. Kirkpatrick said, "I'm so sorry to hear that," while her eyebrows continued to point heavenward in an expression of fierce incredulity.

Mrs. Allende, when asked, also admitted that she was Peruvian by birth. This was the first outright lie she permitted herself. She was determined to keep the fibs to a minimum. When she reached ten, she had already decided, the game would be up and she would spring the truth of her identity on her interlocutor, who would have nowhere to turn as over the mid-Atlantic the seatbelt sign began to flash and the plane to dip unsteadily. Yes, she was Peruvian but she

had lived in many places, she added. She then asked Mrs.
Kirkpatrick casually if she had ever been to Peru or Chile in
the course of her travels. Beyond the lie of omission about
herself, she was pretending not to know who Mrs.
Kirkpatrick was. That ought to count as double forfeits, she
thought, bringing the score to something like five already.
Then she reflected that Mrs. Kirkpatrick for her part had
also failed to present herself in her true colors, as a member
of the United States cabinet with a special interest in Latin
American affairs, the woman who had said shortly before
the Falklands debacle, "Argentina is my favorite country."
She wondered if perhaps Mrs. Kirkpatrick too were not
playing her own little game. She thought not. In any event,
the score stood at five down, five to go.

Mrs. Kirkpatrick replied that she had visited Chile several
times and in fact had been to Santiago and Viña del Mar
only a few months before. Mrs. Allende, at this mention of
the place where they had buried her husband, allowed herself to look somber and wistful and to quote a few lines
from their beloved Neruda, *"Viene el mar y reune nuestras
vidas y . . ."* Here she faltered. Mrs. Kirkpatrick, who was
nothing if not well-read, recognized the line from one of
the poet's late, brief, apolitical works and supplied the
rest—*"y solo ataca y se reparte y canta"*—pleased with the
chance to display an erudition all but wasted on her colleagues in New York and Washington.

What a delightful person, she thought. Perhaps I shall
invite her to dinner in Mexico City. She was headed for
Acapulco where her husband was already waiting to share a
week's vacation, but she planned to spend at least one night
in the capital en route.

They got to talking, naturally enough, about their children. Mrs. Kirkpatrick's sons were taking doctorates, one in
economics, the other in computer science. Mrs. Allende's
daughter was married, she confided, to an economist. She
had just been visiting the children in Geneva.

After lunch had been served and removed, Mrs.

Kirkpatrick took out a briefcase and began reading papers. Mrs. Allende was too well-bred to glance at them over her companion's sholder, although, as she thought in a rare moment of bitterness, she had every right to do so. She took out a book on the Swiss banking system that her daughter had given her and pretended to absorb herself in the chapter dealing with the role of one Swiss bank in the Chilean truckers' strike of 1973, a whole concatenation with which she was only too familiar.

After half an hour, Mrs. Kirkpatrick looked up from her papers and asked her elegant companion if the book she was reading was interesting.

"I pretend to take an interest for the family's sake," Mrs. Allende replied. "My daughter's husband has no small talk, no conversation at all outside his field." She shut the volume and slipped it discreetly into her handbag. "As for myself, I prefer novels and mysteries," she added, hoping to lead the conversation onto a safer path.

"How about a crossword puzzle?" Mrs. Kirkpatrick asked, and pulled one from amid the clutter of papers spread before her. She shoved the rest of the papers back into her briefcase and snapped it shut.

"*Ay, eso sí!*" Mrs. Allende exclaimed. The score now stood at six because of her answer about the book and she had just understood that she had invented the game as a delaying tactic. She dreaded a confrontation in midair. The crossword puzzle might well spare her.

"Peter south of the border, that's easy, *Pedro.*" Mrs. Kirkpatrick wrote in the first definition in ink. "But what about this: Picasso's footgear?"

Mrs. Allende thought for a moment. She was aware only after the answer came to her how badly she had needed the respite offered by a moment of disinterested search. This voyage in first class was proving a torment to her. (She generally traveled cabin class but her daughter had thought she looked tired and insisted on paying for first.)

"A-L-P-A-R-G-A-T-A-S," she spelled out. "I think you call

them espadrilles, which is the French word, I believe. Picasso of course was Catalan."

"I don't know what I'd do without you," Mrs. Kirkpatrick said, and breezed through the rest of the puzzle on her own. Her pleasure in her own cleverness expanded to include her companion, whom she then and there invited to meet her for breakfast the following morning at a bakery in the *Zona Rosa* that both women knew well, a Swiss bakery as it happened.

"We can meet once more on neutral territory then." Mrs. Allende, having ventured this small joke, looked to see her companion's reaction. Mrs. Kirkpatrick gave no sign of having caught the irony. She was saying, out loud to herself, "72 Down, Pinochet to his pals. That's easy. Augusto with two u's, as in English, seven letters, perfect. Finished." She folded the completed puzzle and tucked it into the seat.

"Well, one isn't always this fortunate in one's traveling companions," she said. She liked this woman, this Señora— "What did you say your name was?"

"Alarid," said Mrs. Allende without batting an eyelash. That made seven.

"And mine is Kirkpatrick," said Mrs. Kirkpatrick, forthright, and offered her hand to her seatmate who took it thinking, How she enjoys her incognito, poor thing. I won't deprive her yet of that complex pleasure.

The pleasure was far greater than Mrs. Allende could have suspected. Mrs. Kirkpatrick was ruminating an article she meant to write during her vacation, on just the class of Latin American this handsome agreeable woman represented. It was this class, whose ideal was public service rather than feudal self-aggrandizement, that most nearly mirrored the North American elite to which she herself belonged. It was this class, she would assert in the article, that must be strengthened and encouraged to take charge in Latin America. Of course it really wasn't quite fair to use a chance acquaintance as a guinea pig, a paradigm case, but then Mrs. Kirkpatrick's public position and crowded schedule were such that she had to seize the opportunities as they arose. And it was all to a good purpose that she would exploit Mrs. Alarid's delightful naïveté.

Before breakfast next day they did a little shopping on *calle Londres*. Mrs. Alarid bought a ring for her daughter in Lima (which made eight, thought Mrs. Allende, as her daughter was in Havana) and Mrs. Kirkpatrick bought herself a lacy white shawl to wear in the evenings in Acapulco. Mrs. Alarid bargained fluently with the salesgirl at Mrs. Kirkpatrick's request and obtained a ten-percent discount on the price of the shawl. For the ring she simply paid the first price quoted. Mrs. Kirkpatrick was impressed with the offhand way this widow spent her pesos and decided she must represent very old, very established money.

The other tables in the window of the little Swiss bakery at the corner of *Genova* and *Praga* were empty that morning at eleven. Mrs. Kirkpatrick had prepared certain questions to ask her new friend, hoping the answers in themselves would add up to an article. To begin with, she asked about her education. Mrs. Allende, pouring coffee from the large pot the waitress had just set down, alluded vaguely to preparatory schools taught by nuns, and a university course in literature abandoned in order to devote herself to her family. (Which made nine, as she had taken the same degree as her late husband.)

"And what did your husband do?" Mrs. Kirkpatrick asked. Mrs. Allende looked at her questioner. Was this woman with the slanted foxlike eyes determined to sniff her out? But she would not tell lie number ten yet. She would abide by the rules of the game, but make her revelation when she chose and not before.

"He was in the government at the end," Mrs. Alarid said softly.

"Ah, I see, a bureaucrat or an elected official? Not that there's always much to choose between them. I speak of my own country of course," Mrs. Kirkpatrick quickly amended, doing her best to be deferential and charming. The woman seated across from her, a good family woman, like herself, was a positive gold mine as far as the article was concerned. It was almost too easy. At the university, taking her doctorate, Mrs. Kirkpatrick had spent months researching each paper, knowing it might lie buried for years on some professor's desk. Now her chance observations were printed and broadcast as a matter of course. She longed for a challenge and this woman, dear soul, was a pushover.

"Oh, he was elected, to a very high office. Our country is a democracy." The slip was genuine, and she corrected it at once, determined not to lie again until she was ready to face the consequences. "Our country *was* a democracy."

"What years was he in office?" Mrs. Kirkpatrick marshaled her formidable knowledge of recent Latin American history. There had been those leftish lieutenants in Peru and then elections again only recently. The truth was she had paid rather less attention to Peru, with its inscrutable masses of Indians and messy earthquakes, than to the other southern-tier nations, so much more Europeanized and reliable. She promised herself she would bone up on Peru as soon as she returned to New York.

Mrs. Allende, now convinced that her coffee-klatsch companion had not the slightest idea to whom she was speaking over the stainless steel coffeepot, the thick white cups, and tray of brioches and jams, looked at her with pity and said, "My husband was murdered in the fall of seventy-three."

Mrs. Kirkpatrick dropped her cup into the saucer. The sound of cup striking plate rang in the empty cafe. Coffee splashed onto the snow white tablecloth, scattering pale brown stains in front of her.

"How perfectly awful," she said. "You poor thing. Was it during his time in office, by any chance. Did it have to do with—I hope you don't mind my asking—his political posture? I'm very interested in such things, you see. I hope you don't mind my asking."

"Not at all," said Mrs. Allende, from whom a great weight was suddenly lifted as she understood that for Mrs.

Kirkpatrick she had long ago ceased to exist and never would again. The dreaded revelation would not have been one. Mrs. Kirkpatrick would probably have shrugged.

Mrs. Allende reached for the bill that lay on the table between them and snatched it up and said, "Today, you are my guest." She strode over to the cashier at the counter where the pastries were displayed, those confections to which the Swiss give such quaint names, full of historical reference.

"*Japonaise, Napoléon, diplomate, religieuse,*" she recited to herself, repeating the last antithetical couplet, "*Diplomate, religieuse.*" Having paid the bill she returned to the table, left a tip by her saucer, reached out her hand to Mrs. Kirkpatrick, withdrew it deftly and said, looking straight at her, "*Ha sido Usted tan amable de aclarar cosas que no entendía antes de conocerla.*" This was not a lie. She had learned a great deal from Mrs. Kirkpatrick, while revealing very little. Could this be called a triumph?

At any rate, she was able to walk out of the bakery and past the plate glass window without fearing the other woman's eyes that she knew would be studying her to the last, intently. Not a triumph certainly and yet not a defeat either. She had simply done what the occasion called for.

"*Hola Tencha, te queremos mucho,*" two young Mexican women, students by the look of them, called out to her from the other side of the street. She was startled by the easy recognition, the familiar use of her nickname, frightened to lose the complicated anonymity conferred on her by the American woman she had left behind. But the fear passed quickly. She was herself again and could breathe freely, waiting on the *Paseo de la Reforma* for a taxi to take her home.

At the Border

Abel came to San Martin to be a painter. He had a small income from a trust fund and all the requisite skills. He was a fine draftsman, a graduate of the Amsterdam academy, and the professional collectors of butterflies, birds, and Mayan artifacts who came to chart the *terra incognita* of the San Martin jungle found him a useful collaborator in their sporadic quests. Kept busy by the collectors, enthralled by their minute discoveries of painted shard and splintered bone, it took him some time to realize that if they knew what they were looking for, he did not. Left to himself he had no idea what to paint.

Thinking he might do better in a proper studio, he bought, after the first devaluation, a crumbling adobe fortress in an outlying district of town, and spent several years restoring it to pristine colonial style, with plain squared-off tree trunks for pillars to support the red tile eaves of the deep verandas. The pillars were tarred black to contrast with the whitewashed walls of his domain, his fortress against the world.

In time he became something of a collector himself, making frequent trips across the border, an easy day's drive from San Martin, into the Guatemalan highlands, in search of old weavings to cover the empty walls of his house. In a

115

stream bed in the high Cuchumatanes he found an enormous polished boulder as deeply and mysteriously red as
the dye in the old weavers' yarns. He rolled this stone uphill
through rugged terrain and managed to load it into his van,
caught in a net such as the natives of the region used to
transport their necessities on their backs. To him the stone,
objet trouvé, was a necessity, or why would he have bothered
to cart it all the way back across the border, to the amuse-
ment of Mexican customs officials God had punished by letting them be posted to a concrete shed with a tin roof at the
very bottom of the republic. They made Abel haul the stone
onto their scales—to his amazement it weighed twenty-five
kilos—and threatened to levy an import duty of a thousand
pesos per kilo, making up the law as they went along, which
was one of the consolations of their remote posting.

"I suppose we don't have enough stones in our country to
satisfy you," they said, and "Why didn't you just stay where
you found it." In the end they settled for a small fine as a
sop to their wounded national pride.

With the stone properly positioned on his hearth and the
weavings hung where the sun would not fade them, Abel
was restless again and beset by doubts. The studio at the
back of the house, facing the pear orchard, was not as con-
ducive as he had hoped. Perhaps he lacked a true vocation?
The question tormented him. The refugees, when they arrived, were a kind of solution.

The outlaw government of Guatemala had declared a
state of siege and sent a brutal army of terrified conscripts
into the Cuchumatanes to ransack and raze villages along
the border. The inhabitants were either murdered or put to
rout. Within six months of the declaration, there were sixty
refugee camps on the Mexican side of the border and the
tires on Abel's old van were ready to give out under the
weight of the loads of corn, beans, and blankets he had carried, making two or three trips each week, over unpaved
road and jungle track, to feed the hungry and clothe the
naked.

It is not often one is given the chance to perform an action that is purely and unambiguously useful. Abel knew this and tried hard to prove worthy of the great occasion, just as he had always gone to pains for the passing paleontologists who paid him in kind (a mounted specimen, a sliver of petrified bone) or not at all. He had written, with many discarded drafts, to his mother's wealthy friends in Amsterdam, Paris, and Mexico City, begging them to help. He had even written, breaking a silence of several years' duration, to his father in Tangiers. His father had not answered but had forwarded Abel's letter to a former colleague at the UN in Geneva who had in turn sent it on to the High Commission on Refugees where a supernumerary answered a son's plea to his father with a fat sheaf of illustrated brochures.

"That's just the kind of man he was," Abel told his good friend Piet, a young Jesuit from Antwerp who had also come to San Martin on a collector's quest. Piet was combing the state's colonial archives, a mass of documents unsorted since separation from the mother country and illegible by now to the untrained eye, for mention of local Indian groups that history had submerged. Gifted with the humble persistence of a medieval copyist, he had recorded his findings on several thousand three by five cards in a neat but miniscule hand. Monkish humility combined in him with the Voltairean pride of a debunker of myths. When he published his findings, there would be wailing and gnashing of teeth among his colleagues who had written the history of the Spanish colonies without going as he had to the difficult source.

"Was?" Piet questioned his friend's use of the past tense.

"Was to me," Abel said. "After all I haven't seen my father in ten years." His parents had divorced when he was an infant. He had seen his father half a dozen times since then and received advice he was (his father said) unwilling to follow.

"Don't look at me that way, pardoning me for uncharita-

ble thoughts," Abel said, mostly to tease Piet, who was so
utterly reticent in the exercise of his vocation one couldn't
help but tease him. Whether out of some unfathomable
Jesuit subtlety or to undo, singlehanded, centuries of
church militancy, Piet never referred to matters of faith except in joking or veiled terms. Nothing in his speech or behavior would have revealed his calling to anyone meeting
him for the first time. On the contrary, Abel had come up
from the garden where he was planting rosebushes, and
there in the patio were the roofer, who was supposed to be
mending the roof, and the roofer's wife, who was supposed
to be doing the washing in a stone trough, standing agape
while a stranger too tall and fair to be a native of San Martin marched across the cobblestones on a pair of stilts. The
roofer was unhappy because he had salvaged the stilts from
a rotten beam to take home to his children and didn't want
Abel to know. The roofer's wife was unhappy because she
recognized the clown. She shook the suds from her hands
and crossed herself in dismay at the dancing priest, from
whom she had received communion, she told Abel, only the
day before.

The discovery that they had been born within a few miles
of each other on opposite sides of the Dutch-Belgian border
helped cement their friendship thousands of miles from
home. And then the war had come in Guatemala and the
refugees to San Martin, with their tall tales and credible
signs of horror, and for the first time in his life Abel found
himself making decisions on which other lives depended.
He began to look to Piet not only as an arbiter of the daily
questions—where to send a small allotment of medical sup-
plies, how to spend twenty thousand devalued pesos to feed
twenty thousand people—but to provide, if not a faith, at
least a rationale against despair. Abel did not believe in
God. Neither did he trust the thin iconography of certain
leaflets—bayonets, clenched fists, tilted berets—that had begun to circulate in San Martin, drifting down from the cap-

ital. He believed, now that life without belief had become impossible, in Piet.

It was November, warm, dry, and pleasant. The corn stalks were broken and bent in the fields. The floor of the pine forest was still green after autumn rains. Abel was glad to have Piet as his traveling companion on the week's last run to the border instead of dour Sister Kearney. The old American woman had been working in jungle missions both sides of the border for twenty years and managed to remind Abel anew each time they met how late and tardy were his own efforts. She would never have dreamed of suggesting, as Piet did, that they stop the van only an hour out of town, at the edge of the forest of pine and scrub oak, to partake of a light alfresco lunch. Sister Kearney would have been shocked to see of what the lunch consisted. Piet had brought it all in a knapsack.

"Pâté de foie gras, Camembert, *confitures de mirabelles*. My sister sent it all for the holidays. What do you say to that?"

"Sounds divine," Abel said with private irony. It was the kind of word his mother's friends were free with.

"Not divine, only human," Piet corrected him. "But all the same. I hid the package from my brothers at the mission house. Of course it's not quite the same as at home, but we won't complain." He had spread a large bandana as a table-cloth and was opening the cans with the blade of his Swiss army knife.

"We'll have to supply the entremets from memory: *rôti de porc, au fenouil; poularde de Bresse, moules marinières,* take your pick or have them all." Piet's sea-gray eyes rolled with mock nostalgia at this litany of gastronomic prayers, none of them likely to be answered in the dry upland forest where they sat within view of a stunted herd of grimy sheep tended by two equally grimy children in tunics of dull scratchy wool.

"Don't offer them the pâté," Piet said when he noticed the children staring from behind a rock as he prepared two thick *tartines* like the ones he said his mother always had for him when he returned from school. He beckoned to the children to approach, but they only stared wide-eyed for a second, then turned and bolted, falling over their frightened flock.

"Poor kids don't know what they're missing." Piet offered one of the buttered breads to Abel and bit into the other himself.

"People starving down there at the border and here we sit." Abel waited for Piet to dispel this uncomfortable thought for him.

"Ah," Piet waved the blade that had spread the jam, "the poor ye have always with you."

"Whereas you . . ." the justification for the picnic became clear to Abel as he remembered the rest of the verse, "are going away. Where? When?" After the dry bread and pâté he felt like a force-fed goose opening its beak to squawk. He reached eagerly for the bottle of Argentine *tinto*.

"They're sending me to Los Angeles at the end of this month, next week in fact. I thought we might break bread together one last time. It wasn't my idea to leave so soon, or rather I did ask for this posting but that was two years ago. And I had forgotten about it," he assured Abel, "when the order came. The mills grind slowly."

"You're not unhappy about it." Abel meant it as a question but it sounded more like an accusation addressed to the young man who was carefully folding the green bandana.

"I'm going to learn about computers," Piet spoke the word like the opening notes of a great fugue, and stretched his long fingers as if to pluck the notes on a giant keyboard. "I'll feed all my notes into the computer and it will write my book for me and perhaps the University of California will publish it. In a year, less even, I may be sending you a copy."

"And you," he went on before Abel dared think either a year ahead or a year back, "will send me news of the work and how it's going. I'll worry about you." He clapped a hand on Abel's shoulders as they strolled back across the soft floor of the forest where only the soughing of the wind could be heard. "How much longer can you keep it up? Back and forth, back and forth, and it's only a drop in the bucket. The refugees keep coming." He shook his head at the immensity of human folly.

"We've been through it all so many times." Abel was irritated for some reason. In fact Piet had avoided the painful meetings at which the expatriate colony in San Martin discussed the refugees' futures and their own, now inextricably linked. "The government of the sovereign state of Mexico will make up its mind and allow the UN to take over the camps, or it will throw us all out and seal the border. Meanwhile, Sisyphus can hack it."

Sisyphus was the name Piet had called him after seeing the boulder Abel had rolled uphill from over the border. The boulder was still sitting on Abel's hearth and only an earthquake could dislodge it from there.

"I'd forgotten about Sisyphus. *Je ne croyais pas si bien dire,*" Piet said, and broke into a run to make up for the time stolen from their pressing errand or, as Abel rather thought, for the sheer pleasure of running whether anyone could keep up with him or not, and if they couldn't so much the better. There was, he had noticed before, a lot of show-off in Piet. He thought sadly, as he walked back to the van, not trying to catch up, that if the two of them had met at home as children they would probably have detested one another on sight.

Abel's Uncle Joos had hidden a Jewish family in the basement of his house in Amsterdam until the spring of 1944 when they were betrayed and shipped east in that last busy season in hell. Uncle Joos was sent to work in a factory in Darmstadt and when he came home at the war's end he packed his bags and left the Old World for good. To Abel growing up, his uncle was a legend, a promise of escape from those heavy family dinners at which over coffee and brandy the horrors of the recent past were retold in predictable sequence.

When he arrived in San Martin, following his uncle's trajectory, he found that the old man, nearing seventy by then, had just married a young woman from an outlying village and brought her to live with him in town, in two squalid rooms in a house shared by several families. The sight of the unkempt old man, dressed in knickers and heavy boots like a colonial explorer, keeping house with a girl of twenty who stood at the stove peeling potatoes, letting the peel drop to the floor, shocked and revolted the fastidious young man Abel had become. Magda smiled at him distractedly and warmed her hands over the steaming pot.

His uncle took Abel into their other room, poured him a glass of some awful sweet liqueur of local manufacture and told him, "Magda is blind. In her village she was therefore considered undesirable and would hever have found a husband. I married her to give her a chance in life. Our children will have a good education. And she will never see their faces. I am not blind, by the way. I can see right into your head but that's all right. Charity begins at home." He thumped his chest and settled himself more comfortably on his narrow nuptial bed. "You don't have to finish your glass. It's made from fermented blackberries and rubbing alcohol."

Magda came to Abel's house, picked up every object her hands encountered, patting it greedily all over, and demanded to know in a shrill singsong voice what he had paid for it and to whom. Conscious of having risen in the only world she knew, she aped the awful manners of the class San Martin considered above hers, that of the small shopkeepers who stayed in business by swindling their Indian customers out of small sums, persistently. Joos was robust and stubborn and full, Abel learned, of theories about local history he was ready to expound to anyone who would buy him a drink. He spent his evenings in bars and cafes holding forth to European tourists and when these were not available, to Americans. Magda did not complain. She boasted to Abel that no matter how drunk Joos got he never beat her or let the children go hungry.

The children were now old enough to walk on their own feet. Magda, with Joos guiding her elbow, had carried them for years, barely aware of their weight or presence. Whatever his plans for their education, Joos left them entirely to her care. Their faces were not often washed or their hair combed. They spoke three languages (but all Indian children spoke two, their own and Spanish) and would understand the world better than he did by the time they were his age, Abel believed. They had beautiful round pale smudged faces. They had never gone hungry.

Much as he mistrusted Joos, considered him both hypocrite and fool, when Abel had spent an afternoon with the two children, making them a kite or sketching horses to amuse them, he conceded to his uncle some kind of blind wisdom or foolish courage he knew was missing in himself. When he tried to question his uncle about the years just after the war when Joos had traveled—so Abel had been told as a child—to a hundred fifty countries, the best he could get from the old man was a lecture on the use of tonal inflections in Indonesian and Mexican dialects. *"Acapoolco,"* he crooned, diagramming the shifts in pitch on a paper napkin. Abel learned from others that Joos was supporting Magda's entire clan with money sent him by friends at home. Of course Joos too was now a member of Magda's clan and lived unabashedly on the kindness of friends, but simply, still in the same subdivided house where he and Magda rented three rooms now instead of two, because of the children. His uncle's messy life had frightened and repelled Abel until he began to serve as courier to the refugee camps. Now it was order he despised, the bureaucratic sense of order that quarantined the refugees to a narrow no-man's land along the dangerous border. The descent oppressed him.

Not so Piet, who was excited and stimulated by the transition, accomplished in under three hours, from cold piney uplands to the promiscuous heat of the dense jungle. It was for this he had left his teaching position at the Jesuit college in Antwerp. Flat country, flat predictable lives of the upper bourgeoisie who sent their sons to him to learn the history of the Counter Reformation. San Martin had not disappointed him, especially in these last six months that had brought all the excitement of a revolution and none of the danger. And if the danger should arrive, if those who called the refugees revolutionaries and the relief workers fomentors of revolution should gain the upper hand in San Martin, why he would be long gone by then. Not that he feared danger, dared refuse martyrdom, but since he had to leave, he was just as glad not to leave under pressure of threat, not to confront, just yet, with so much important research unpublished, the question of whether he were a coward.

Adjusting the surplice over his shirt and jeans he approached a clearing away from the ragged rows of tents and half-built huts and ran his eye over the crowd of refugees and poor dirt farmers from the nearest Mexican hamlets and estimated a turnout of about five hundred souls. And where in Europe and when, even if he lived to be named cardinal as his mother predicted, would he have the chance to bring consolation to so many of the faithful in such deep need? One would have to go back to the early missionaries: las Casas, the old bishop who converted the ancestors of these very folk, Sahagún, Landa, and Padre Kino of course, the Jesuit who built the California missions. He tried to imagine the terror, the upheaval, the promise of those early times in the New World. His heart went out to the men who first preached the gospel of peace in the Americas, and to the decimated populations somehow able to receive the message everything they saw with their own eyes belied: slavery, massacre, entire libraries pitched onto the pyre. He knelt before the altar that was only a board resting on two stumps and thanked God for permitting him to witness the recent terrible events in Guatemala so that he might understand, as he never would have otherwise, those early missionaries whose lives, he was sure of it now, would furnish a brilliant first chapter to his book.

Abel mistrusted ritual and mistrusted himself for so doing. He had an idea that his failure as a painter was somehow bound up with this question. Believing in nothing, accepting nothing from tradition, he was obliged to start from scratch, out of his own emptiness. He was, Piet told him, like a sheep in the forest on a very short tether. Since he had no intention of taking part in the service, he stood aside, half hidden behind a tree. As always in this part of the world, the nodding, keening, ecstatic faith of another race left him feeling uncomfortably like a voyeur. Resisting an impulse to move out of earshot, he trained his eyes on Piet and was relieved when the thought came to him that faith was only a series of artfully conjoined reflecting mirrors, placed so as to magnify the light from a single candle, from one good man.

The crowd knelt in the dirt and in the dirt kept upright the tiny candles they had brought to the clearing. When Piet had first seen the masses of skinny candles on the stone floors of the Guatemalan churches, an indispensable accompaniment to prayer, he assumed they were a pagan vestige, a mild form of idolatry. Now he saw further: the candles were only a symbol of the inner light to which he, the priest, could provide a mirror, giving each man and woman in the crowd of victims a vision of all the lights at once, as one. This was the mystery of communion, of community. And behind it lay the still greater mystery of a faith brought to this place by soldiers' greed and carelessness and revivified through centuries by soldiers obeying orders.

On the return trip they were too tired to talk but when they reached the edge of the plateau that sloped gently upward toward San Martin, and the evening chill began to seep from the woods into the emptied van, Piet began, predictably, to sing in Flemish, a slow melancholy ballad of the South African veldt.

"For God's sake, sing something more cheerful if at all," Abel protested. By the time they had reached the first unpaved marginal streets of the town, they were into the sixth verse of a French drinking song about a shepherdess and four pretty boys by the river, and it was just repetitive enough and inane enough to carry the weight of their conjoined and private griefs. Some things are best defined by what they are not. The last verse brought them across the patio of Abel's house and into the room Piet had been using as study and repository for books and papers, there being no room for such elaborate pursuits at the mission house across town where he boarded gratis. This room had been Abel's share in his work and it was Abel therefore, as host, who felt obliged to interpret what confronted them.

"They must have been looking for money, or checks," he said. It was amazing what a large area the file cards covered, spilled from the shoeboxes where Piet had packed them too tightly, a visible metaphor of his effort to compass the unknown past.

"Thanks be I'm getting out of here," he said and fell to his knees among the debris of his work. Some of it had been torn into many small pieces. The rest was simply crumpled or trodden underfoot. So much paper, Abel thought. In the fireplace it would have burned for hours.

"Not a theft." Piet said. "A warning, a vengeance perhaps. How close it cuts."

"A warning to whom?" Abel asked.

"To us all," Piet said absently, searching among the papers for his notes from the Seville archive. But the rest of the house had not been disturbed. In Abel's studio the easel stood where he had placed it one afternoon the preceding May, in order to catch a certain light through the pear tree blossom. Nothing had been touched since.

"Whoever it was, they knew they couldn't get to me that way. They seem to know I don't give a damn about any of this any more." Abel laughed till he cried and it was of no use for Piet to protest.

"Someday you will. If not here, perhaps in another place—"

"What other place?" Abel stopped him cold. "Do you think I can just cut and run too? I live here. My family is here." He thought of Joos and Magda's children.

"This is very bad." Piet couldn't stop shaking his head like an old man. Even this irritated Abel now. Couldn't he feel an emotion without projecting it, dramatizing it. A priest was only an actor after all, in a horrendous inhuman comedy.

"Come on," he said to Piet at last. "Let me help you pick it all up. Maybe it's not as bad as it looks."

"Please, no." Piet recoiled as if Abel had proposed something unclean. "I'll do it all myself. I have it all in my head, the plan, the program. Just let me be for now."

He was just like the other collectors Abel had known. Well, why shouldn't he love his old facts from dead hands? He was only human after all, like the pâté and the jam, not divine, only human.

"All right, I'll keep out of your way. Take your time." Abel found himself out in the street once again. He climbed wearily into the van, in which he had already spent so much of the day, and drove across town and up Low Hill to see if Hilda and Curley were all right. That was how he put it to himself. It was easier to imagine their need than to admit his own.

Of course they were all right. It was Abel they worried about, these two expatriates from the west coast of the United States of North America. They had already been in San Martin for fifteen years when Abel arrived and they had taken him under their wing at once.

"You look like you lost your best friend," Curley, the sensitive one, said when she had let him into the living room. A fire burned in the tall white fireplace. There were large vases of flowers in both bay windows and the table was set for two.

"Of course he does," Hilda snapped. "He was down there

again today. Was it awful?" She lowered her voice. "Any
deaths?" She was the tough one. Bad news didn't scare her.

They had come to San Martin to photograph the natives
and had stayed to grumble about them, humorously or with
bitter indignation. Their hilltop dwelling suited them, everyone said, like a shell secreted about them. There was a
darkroom, a handsome veranda where Martha Washington
geraniums climbed the red brick pillars, an enormous vege-
table garden so they needn't go to market more than once a
week, and then only if company were coming to dinner.

Within this little enclave they lived carefully and they
lived well and they could no longer imagine living anywhere
else, certainly not on their small pensions. The greatest fear
of each was that she might outlive the other. Curley was the
more delicate also in appearance, small, slender, white
haired, with a sharp chin and bright eyes and a wardrobe of
toreador pants and frilly shirts, which careful laundering by
a succession of well-trained help had kept intact since the
late 1950s when she had last been gainfully employed as a
high-school teacher in San Francisco. Her health was not
good and her evening reading tended toward philosophical
tracts Abel had not known were to be found in San Martin:
Death: The Better Part of Life or *Thanatology: The Gay Science.*

Hilda looked sturdier but one knew she was afflicted with
slow angers, gnawing grudges against former residents of
San Martin who by the very fact of being former, fed her
tenacious rancors. To leave town, once she had accepted
you into her circle, conceded you "the right texture" for San
Martin, was a betrayal, a defection she could never forget.
There was the couple from New York who had come to San
Martin to save their marriage and having saved it had left
again without giving Hilda the old fridge they promised
her. There was the reporter from Zurich who hired Hilda
to photograph a celebrated village fiesta and never paid for
the work. There was the . . . Abel knew the list by heart.

He also knew that Hilda loved him because she was sure
of him. He would never defect, default, abscond. San Mar-

tin was his life as it was hers. She had given instructions, to an undertaking establishiment in the state capital, that on her death she was to be cremated and the ashes strewn in the Grijalba river from the promontory where four centuries before an entire nation, men, women, and children, were said to have leapt to their deaths rather than submit to enslavement by the Spanish invader. Abel, kind gallant Abel, had promised to see to it all for her when the time came.

"It wasn't as bad as last time I was there," he answered Hilda's questions. He had decided not to mention the break-in at his house. Why disturb before it was absolutely necessary the tranquility of this place of refuge? "Piet played soccer with some of the kids after Mass. They didn't want to let him go."

"Now he doesn't want to see those tonight, Hilda," Curley scolded her friend who was ostentatiously examining some photographs laid out on a bench. "He's had quite enough for one day." Whereby Abel knew these were the pictures Hilda had shot a month earlier, at the border. Curley said, "Soccer, eh? There's nothing our versatile Jesuit can't do."

"I can think of a few things," Hilda objected impishly. She was fond of Piet but her anticlericalism predated their acquaintance by half a century. Besides, both women liked to make their guest of the moment feel he was their favorite, hoping, perhaps unconsciously, that their show of exclusive loyalty would be reciprocated. In short they had become, after so many years in the Mexican provinces, a pair of small-town gossips.

Abel was not unwilling to gossip. It was only fair exchange for the toast and tea and canned sardines they put before him. "Piet is leaving San Martin next week," he announced, because he needed their sympathy and because he was curious to see how the news would strike them.

"He certainly picked a fine time." Hilda was indignant. She had gathered the photos together and put them inside a large folder and was tying it slowly. She waited for Abel to beg her to open it again.

"He didn't pick it," Abel said. "He received an order from his provincial in Antwerp. They're sending him to California. Don't you ever wish . . ." He hesitated. He had been going to say, "that someone would order us away from here." Instead he said, "It must simplify life, taking a vow of obedience."

Curley said wisely, "We all do, you know, but most of us don't make our vows to constituted authority. We are all slaves to something. I'm a slave to three little pills of different colors three times a day."

"I don't think Piet thinks of himself as a slave," Abel said speculatively. His anger had gone. He felt himself being drawn into something too comfortable, too cozy, small-town miasma. Probably even in the camps people gossiped. What else was there to do? But Hilda and Curley were good people. Hilda had solicited and received a money order from a cousin in the States, which she now handed over to Abel. No one would order him away from San Martin. He would cash the check, buy more corn and canned milk and penicillin if he could get it and make another run to the border.

"He admires Piet," Curley said to Hilda. They spoke of Abel in his presence as if he were a small boy who didn't know his own mind. And like a small boy in love with contradiction for its own sake he said, "No, I don't." He thought but did not say, "I love him."

"We happen to think you are the hero of this never-ending tale of woe," Curley said. "I mean, just look what you've accomplished, how many people depend on you."

Having failed to malign Piet they were trying a little flattery on him instead, Abel thought. At other times he had not resisted the blandishments of these two elderly sirens who called themselves, with sour good humor, the two Disgraces, but tonight he was in no mood.

"You spoil me," he protested. "I come barging in here

covered with dust and you ply me with food." He stood up and moved to the doorway.

"We're the ones who are grateful to you," Curley corrected him. "You know we can't forget that it's our government supplying the helicopters and guns and poison gas across the border. Thank heaven we're too old and too poor to pay taxes. I wrote my congressman again today. I'm still an American citizen after all. If I've chosen to live outside my country it's because . . ." Here she faltered, seeming about to dissolve before a stern jury that had called her to account for her defection.

"It's none of his damn business," Hilda said. She meant the congressman's. "We don't owe any explanations," she added with admirable truculence. "As we say at home, it's a free country." They all laughed at this although Abel thought the phrase must have a bitter savor now for the two old American women trapped on the Central American border.

By nine at night San Martin was shuttered, barred, locked, and dark. Turning the heavy iron key in the lock of the heavy wooden door, Abel reentered his beleaguered fortress and withdrew his mail from the box on the inside of the door. Within the house a light burned. Poor Piet was still at it then, rewriting history as best he could with no help from anyone. Abel crossed the patio and let himself into the kitchen quietly so as not to disturb his friend. He opened his two letters.

The first was from his sister, with a program of her last concert in Leyden. The Mozart quintet called for a second viola. He recognized the player's name, that of a young woman he had asked to marry him some years before, when his sister had brought her to San Martin and the three of them had toured the ruins up north together. Antje had seemed surprised when Abel asked her to stay on, and he saw only then that he had mistaken her infatuation with the scenery for something more personal. She was still using the same last name, he noticed from the program. That was the custom now of course. Not that it mattered whether she like himself had remained unattached.

The other envelope was thick and square and addressed in his mother's large hand. It contained another check, the third since August, and a scrawled note, *"Pour vos pauvres."* She regarded the refugees, all sixty thousand of them, as a hobby of his, something to keep him from mischief or melancholy or worse, this runaway son his mother was glad to humor since she could afford to, and besides she felt, Abel knew, even at this late date, that she owed it to him.

The Actor

Paul was always a peaceful child, on the chubby side and not very tall for his age. Perhaps because of his build he cultivated a talent for repartee and disarmed the opposition, such as it was, with a joke or shrug. This method saw him through high school in a small southwestern town without incident. Shortly after graduation, however, he was drafted and sent east to Texas for basic training. Both his father and his father's father had been infantry soldiers in their time and wounded in combat. As a child Paul, with his father's encouragement, had always sworn he would run away rather than fight in a dumb war. But when Paul's father was alive the boy led a sheltered life and dreamed all sorts of things that later, with his father gone, proved impossible. When the call came he remembered his childish vow and quickly put it aside. At eighteen he entered the army.

Basic training in the hot flat plain of western Texas was nearly over when Paul was summoned to the company commander's office one day and introduced to an old man wearing the uniform of a new recruit. His hair was dark, his bearing erect but his face was a ruin.

"This is the actor," the captain said to Paul. "He is preparing to play the role of a soldier in an important production. We want you to show him around. He'll ask you a lot of questions and your job will be to answer to the best of your abilities. Now that there's a war on it's important we be well-represented on the home front by men like him. So help him to help yourself. Dismissed."

Paul saluted only a second ahead of the actor who, a quick study, could already mimic to perfection the inclination of his hand, the elevation of his elbow. The two returned to the barracks together, the actor close on the heels of his assigned model. At the opening of the tent Paul turned and said, as he might have to the kid sitting behind him in math class a few months earlier:

"Hey, whatever you're looking for, I haven't got it."

The actor stopped in his tracks and Paul wondered for an instant if the man had anything at all to say for himself or if, since he seemed at a loss for words, he was helpless without a script.

"Did anyone ever tell you that you come down harder on your right foot than your left?" the actor asked. "Why is this do you suppose?" At which Paul understood that he himself was to provide the script. At that, he rebelled.

"I don't know why the captain picked on me. I'm not a soldier, I've only been in the army eight lousy weeks. I have my whole life ahead of me."

"So do we all," the actor said mildly. Paul was chastened by this remark. He was delicate enough to see that he had said the wrong thing to a man who appeared, in fact, to have his whole life behind him, a man with wheezing breath and trembling vowels. At second glance his dark hair appeared to be dyed.

"Were you ever in the movies?" Paul asked deferentially and to change the subject. He had always been a great one, his mother said, for changing the subject.

"Before you were born," the actor winked. "But to get back to business. I'll bet your right foot is a whole size larger than your left. Odd, isn't it?"

Paul lifted his right foot in its regulation army boot as if to give the old man a kick but it was clear to them both that never for anything in the world would he actually have done so.

The men in Paul's company had been debating their chances of being sent overseas to fight. The appearance in their midst of the aging thespian was taken as an encouraging sign. If as he insisted without being asked he was a member of the ranks with no privilege of any sort, then it was unlikely they were destined for combat duty in the near future. The actor was clearly too old and frail to fight. So delicate in fact that the company took to treating him as a sort of talisman or mascot. They were as protective of him as they hoped their superiors would be of them when the time came.

And then there was his aura of celebrity. None of them had heard of him before he showed up but they were modest enough, and eager enough for diversion from their exhausting routine, to credit rumors that he had once been a big name in the movies. They gave him star treatment, admired qualities in him they took for granted or would have condemned in themselves. He was a good sport, they said, to join the army at his age. He was lucky, they joked, to be so deaf he couldn't hear shots fired in rifle practice. They did many of his daily tasks for him and he accepted their help, graciously and without embarrassment, as his due. In the barracks there were no secrets. They knew that he wore rouge and dyed his hair and that a corset compressed his waist and hips into a semblance of youthful slimness and vigor. But so what? It takes all kinds, they said, and challenged him again to an arm-wrestling match and were delighted when he won.

Paul was too smart to interfere with this state of affairs although for his own part he found the actor, who continued to shadow him mercilessly, a dangerous nuisance. The nuisance was there from the start. The danger became clear during war games at the end of basic training. The actor took part in these as befitted one of his calling. He had a stand-in for the messy parts. The stand-in was Paul. The

Reds and the Blues were chasing each other through ten square miles of snake-infested Texas bottomland. Sent to scout in Blue territory, Paul had just managed to crawl on his belly through dense underbrush, had staggered to his feet and was wiping the sweat from his brow when the actor called out to him, from the high ground, like a football coach in a movie:

"Attaboy, you're doing just fine." Thus alerting the enemy to Paul's presence. They began to shoot. He stumbled on through the swamp thinking that had the blanks just fired been real bullets he would now be lying wounded or dead. No, the actor was no guarantee of his safety. He was more like an exemplary punishment, an extra forty pounds of gear to haul.

The captain knew what he was doing when he chose Paul to be the actor's aide. By the time the boy reached Red headquarters his anger had faded and when he saw the actor sitting coolly at a table where the staff sergeant was explaining a map, he was able to hold his tongue. But he decided to see the captain and ask for a transfer to another unit.

The actor showed his gratitude to the rest of the company by putting on a little show at the end of basic training. The men had become so used to their mascot that they were surprised, the night of the performance, to find him surrounded by the trappings of his trade. Not that he didn't remain perfectly at ease under the heavy stage makeup in which they now saw him for the first time. But who would have thought that he, whom they had invested with so many imaginary qualities, could in fact command all those long trucks, the crew of rushed assistants, heavy wires, lamps, cameras, even a portable kitchen to feed the hands, a small army within the army, as it were.

Before the performance began in the mess hall, with the tables pushed back to serve as benches where the men sat swinging their legs and drinking soda from cans, the actor addressed his audience.

"Now don't be disappointed if you don't see yourselves on TV next week. It will take time to complete the film. You know," he went on, pausing long enough to mark the seriousness of the proposition he was about to introduce, in the manner of a man whose patience has been tried and found ample, "being in a movie is a lot like being in the army. Most of the time you stand around and wait your turn to be shot. And when your turn does come at last they tell you, not always very kindly, that you've done it all wrong, so you wait some more and do it over and over till you're plain sick of it."

"What about the love scenes?" a soldier in the back row shouted.

"Well, to tell the truth now," the old actor continued in the same slow earnest rhythm, "I never got to do a whole lot of those. You see, I was not generally a leading man. I was never the guy who got the girl or even the guy who lost the girl. I was a character actor." And he explained that you could always tell the characters from the heroes because at the end of the movie the former were as they had been at the beginning while the latter had either won or lost.

"Where does that leave us?" It was Paul who asked and although all eyes were trained on the actor so that no one noticed who had spoken, he blushed bright red.

"In real life, in the life I've been privileged to share with you these past few weeks," the actor said with gravity while Paul wondered if this were then a farewell performance, "I have had a chance to see that there is not one of you who hasn't got the makings of a hero."

Silence met this remark that only a few days before would probably have aroused embarrassment or derision. That morning as the movie vans were arriving in camp the company assembled on the parade ground had been informed that they were soon to be sent overseas into the very theater of operations.

"Will you be going with us?" another young man asked.

Now that his ineffectiveness was proved, the troops still clung to their mascot.

"As a matter of fact, since you happen to ask"—the actor again prefaced his message with a string of empty words that gave him a chance, Paul thought, to stun his audience the way a mosquito does its prey—"I expect a decision on that by tomorrow. Needless to say I would consider it a great honor." This too was accepted in thoughtful silence.

Before going on leave Paul asked to speak to the captain, who complimented him on his fine job with the actor. Paul bided his time waiting for the right moment to bring up the matter of his transfer.

"I pride myself on being a good judge of men. I chose you and you were the right man," the captain said as if the credit for putting up with the actor belonged to him rather than to Paul. "That's why I'm sure it will all work out when you go overseas. I wasn't in favor at first to tell the truth. You scored so high on the mechanical aptitude tests we were going to send you for more training in vehicle mainte-nance but the actor convinced me he needs more time with you in the field. And of course I can see his point. Up to now it's all been fun and games and a few mosquitoes. On the other hand if anything should happen to him we'd all look pretty bad. So you'll be stationed in the rear where you shouldn't have too much trouble looking after him. I'm counting on you, son."

The captain was easily old enough to be Paul's father. Now there was much about the filial relation that was strange to Paul, perhaps because his own father had died before he was old enough to think steadily about such things. The captain's offhand use of a paternal form of ad-dress was enough to disarm him. He couldn't bring himself after all to request the transfer. But in that case he might at least ask a question. No one could accuse him of insubor-dination.

"Why does he have to be so old?" Paul asked, making no attempt to hide his distaste. The captain smiled.

"That's easy," he said. "Use your head. Imagine a younger guy, one close to your age, say, in his position. What would the reaction have been in the tents? Besides, it happens that your age cohort is a lean one. We haven't got a player to spare."

His words put Paul in mind of a full chessboard and left no doubt as to which of the pieces he was meant to represent.

Paul didn't tell his mother or his sister about the actor. Every time he looked around, one of them was gazing at him as if for the last time.

"I'm not dead yet, Mom," he finally said one day.

"If they'd send me in your place I'd go tomorrow." His sister was furious that the brutal prehistoric division of the sexes could prevail this late in the twentieth century. "I may sign up anyway. Accidents aren't important."

"By the time you're our age," Paul said, "sex is no longer an accident. That's the way things are."

"I wouldn't be so resigned in your place." His sister was still angry.

"Who says I'm resigned?" Paul asked. "Nothing will happen to me. I can take care of myself." But what about the actor? There he was less certain. But he kept this fear from his kid sister who stared at him across a divide whose measure she took now for the first time. Born a year apart they had done everything together from infancy. When she began to say her own name, it was both their names run together, me an' Paul.

"I'm not just thinking of you, you know," she nagged him. "This war is not something you ought to be mixed up in. I could never take part in it, that's for sure."

"A minute ago you were ready to enlist." He had been teasing her since before either could speak in whole sentences.

"I didn't say on which side I'd like to enlist," she answered him back. She could argue rings around him. They both knew that. And yet she was in awe of him now. Life had claimed him and left her untapped, at large, useless.

He went with her to a friend's house where several girls were meeting to do some sewing. One of the girls was supposed to have had a crush on him the year before, but nothing had come of it. He went in now to say hello to her just in case. The girls were making costumes for the chorus of the school play.

"We thought you'd be in uniform," one of the girls greeted him. It was her bedroom, a girl's bedroom with a blue rug and curtains and a desk too small for her by now where she did her homework with pencils that had tassels on them.

His sister shot the girl an angry look. The year before, she had said to this girl, jostling her in the school corridor between classes, "I don't see what you see in him."

"I have to polish the buttons," Paul said. "If they catch me wearing a uniform with dull buttons I could be court-martialed. There's a war on, you know."

"Really?" The girl seemed to want to believe him. Paul could tell she was trying to imagine how he would look in uniform.

"As long as you're here make yourself useful," his sister said sharply and began to tack a long panel of white gauze over his shoulder. "You make a good dressmaker's dummy," she conceded, being careful however, not to stick him with her pins. "Lucky for us you lost weight in the army."

"I gained but it's all muscle now," he said. "Don't talk back, you might swallow a pin." And he held up his arms in response to a brief gesture from her. She had cloaked him in a sort of toga or chiton over his sweater and jeans.

"Now stand on this chair so I can check the hemline," she ordered. He was her brother and he obeyed, first removing his sneakers, attacking the heel of each with the toe of the other, like the well-brought-up child he was.

"How do you like it?" she asked him after the other girls had acclaimed her skill at draping the fabric.

"It's prickly," he said, while she fussed with the hem. He closed his eyes and waited patiently for her to be done. He was in no hurry. He would have been happy to stay in that upstairs room with its carpet, among the girls with their trinkets and earrings and stuffed toys and lacrosse sticks.

"All right, you can go now," his sister said at last. She pressed a hand to the top of his head, obliging him to bend at the knees so she could lift off the pinned garment without rending it. "You'd just be bored with us."

"Who knows?" Paul said, looking at the girl who was supposed to have had the crush on him.

"He could stay, it doesn't bother me, on the contrary," she said.

Paul slowly pulled a last pin out of his sweater and laid it on the table.

"Go," his sister said at last. It wasn't jealousy that prompted her to dismiss him. "You don't belong here."

On his last day of home leave Paul received in the mail a large glossy black-and-white photo of the actor wearing a suit and smiling hard. He examined it but did not show it to anyone. Either the photo was long out of date or it had been retouched to remove the wrinkles and slack jaw he knew only too well. That night after he had finished packing his duffel bag he took the photo from between the Guinness Book of World Records for 1989 and the Baseball Encyclopedia and looked at it again. The hatred he was supposed to have felt for the swinging dummy during bayonet practice had always eluded him but the coaching made him watchful of himself. Now he was ashamed of the pleasure he took in tearing the photograph into many small pieces. He threw the scraps into a small metal wastebasket decorated with bust portraits of the first thirty-two presidents of the United States. Cleaning his room next day his mother found the scraps and spent a feverish hour piecing them together, as if hoping to read her son's future from the re-assembled portrait. But she had always been given to nervous superstition.

At the end of the sandy beach a row of large gray rocks jutted into the sea. Paul had been posted here since before daybreak to defend the narrow beach from an enemy landing. His position on the outermost rock was immensely vulnerable if a landing should occur and just for that reason he had come to believe, after many months, that it would never take place. His mind was on the last letter that had reached him from his sister. She had recently entered college and wrote of the many wonderful friends she had made. One could talk to them about anything. For example, they had discussed Paul's situation for hours on end and agreed with her that he ought to desert. This suggestion, as far from the realm of the possible as Paul was from home, did not anger or even irritate him. His sister had never taken his view of things. He had understood that from an early age, before such words as "view of things" had a meaning for him. They scarcely had one now. He could not imagine the source of his sister's cosmic bitterness. He lived first of all by a sense of his own capacities. The world fit itself into place around them like the twig a caged chimpanzee grabs through the bars and uses to spear a banana. Paul's quick grasp of the lay of the land for example had made him useful time and again on hikes into the interior the captain had ordered to give the men some respite from the monotony of their narrow beach encampment. If he had been at home now, standing in the doorway of his sister's room, Paul might have answered her, "But I like the army. It's fun in a way. I'm good at it too so far."

To tease her from this distance would not only have been cruel it would have required a greater effort than the day, the rocks, the flat, windless sea, the climbing sun warranted. When he wrote, he decided, he would tell her about some caves he had discovered on their last trek into the hills.

Twenty yards within he had discovered, digging in desultory fashion with his toe, a curved shard formed in the shape of an animal's paw. He had kept it and would give it to his sister on his return home. Let her show it off to her new friends.

The actor woke where he lay in the diminishing shadow of the rocks and made his way cautiously out to Paul. Letting himself down beside the young man, he waited for him to speak. The months of inactivity had brought a change in their relation. It had occurred to Paul that the actor must be, if not an outright impostor, then an irreversible has-been, a two-bit player clearly expendable from the life of the theater he was free to abandon for months at a time. In his thoughts Paul referred to the old actor now as the has-been, the never-was. Out loud he was sometimes rude to him, made fun of his unsure gait, his peeling sunburn, his petty vanity. The actor listened with his head cocked (favoring his good ear, Paul thought with malice) and returned soft words for harsh ones. Then Paul, feeling ashamed and guilty, would start in on him all over again.

"When does your play open, you never did tell me," he asked now. The midday sun made him uncomfortable in his heavy uniform. The actor smiled as if he hadn't heard.

"I just heard up there that the landing is expected tonight, after sundown," he told Paul. "Go back and get some sleep while you can." Paul shuddered despite the heat, stood up, and scanned the horizon. Far down the beach he saw his replacement striding slowly across the sand.

In his tent that afternoon Paul wrote the letter to his sister differently than he had planned. He had intended to dazzle her with the allure of strange sights he had seen: limestone caves, waterfalls, green parrots on the wing and even, one chill morning when fog drifted across the upper slopes of a mountain some miles inland, a pair of courting quetzal birds. Instead he found himself enumerating in nervous haste random details of their common childhood: the cat's favorite pillow, the frog they had found one summer with an extra leg growing from his bloated belly, the fad of wearing sweatshirts inside out, the scars they had given each other in the years when it was still permitted to touch. He was amazed at how fluent and far-reaching his memory was, taking him beyond his own childhood into a past he had neither known nor until this moment wondered about, his father's. His sister probably knew it all already. She was the one who pored over the old photographs; who, assigned in history class to interview "an older person," had pressed her father with questions. "How long were you in the army? Did you kill anyone? Did it hurt when you got shot?" Locking the answers away in the Pandora's box of her memory. But now Paul, the plodder, the incurious self-willed dreamer, found the answers to a thousand questions he had never thought to ask and he was rescued from the assault of all this knowledge only by the loud call from outside the tent, to prepare to meet the enemy.

The actor was right there beside him. They shared a large damp crevice behind some rocks halfway up a hill overlooking the beach. Paul would gladly have dispensed with his company although he couldn't say whom he would have preferred in the actor's place. The old man's attentions had cut him off from the rest of their unit. He had no real buddies. As if realizing this the actor now seemed to be making an effort for Paul's sake and whether by some trick of his craft or simply because the light was nearly gone, he looked younger now than ever before.

"Were you ever in a real battle before?" Paul asked, hoping the man would at least have sense to duck when ducking was called for.

"There is no one in my profession who can't use a refresher course from time to time," the actor replied. Paul had barely time to note the evasive quality of this remark when the first rounds of fire were exchanged. The enemy, contrary to expectations, had planes too. From up the hill antiaircraft guns were being fired. A streak of light, a slow comet's tail, ran into the sea, illuminating, before it vanished, the decks of a long ship just offshore.

"I'm still here," Paul thought by and by. "Tomorrow I may even enjoy thinking over what I've seen tonight." He was too young and too untried to imagine a progression from bad to worse. There was a lot of deafening noise, flashing lights, an enormous and constantly startling spectacle. Paul felt as if he and the other men stationed about the beach were extraneous to the clumsy ballet of great vulnerable machines of the sea and the air. As if to dispel this notion, a shell burst just behind him. The force of the explosion knocked him flat. His head struck the rock that had been his cover. The actor sprang to his feet in apparent disregard for his own safety and ran to Paul's side. He knelt and lifted the boy's head and prompted him in an urgent whisper to keep going. Then Paul understood why the actor had remained with him all these months. He had been waiting—with the thorough dedication to his craft of a true professional, a great performer—for this very moment. Paul understood but he didn't care for already he could see himself as a small figure on a distant stage and his death when it came, came to someone else, while he had taken his place down in the pit, with the rest of the audience.

An Imaginary Line

Living so near the border makes us loopy. We take it for granted. We forget it's not an imaginary line. That's why when the embassy in Mexico City wouldn't give Roberto a visa, despite his twelve years in prison and his brother waiting to see him in Roswell, we thought we'd just go over and take him across in the back of our car. Julio, the brother living here, didn't like the plan.

"Imagine," he said, "if you get caught. They'd put him in those hideous orange overalls that glow in the dark. I don't think my brother could take any more of that."

Roberto did his twelve at Libertad prison in Montevideo. He was never covicted of a crime because he never stood trial but on his record the charge reads in one loaded word: conspiracy. In Latin America in the early seventies people were saying, Watch out, now that the U.S. is out of Vietnam they'll have more time for us, and then the dominoes fell, Chile, Uruguay, Argentina, until it almost seemed as if those irritating pundits knew what they were talking about. (The worst thing about living with the U.S. is that it skews everyone else's view of their own country; it dulls their self-critical faculties, which are the ones a country needs most.)

The idea for our escapade (we clung to that word because it's cognate with escape) came from Janice, or Dr. Brown as she calls herself when dealing with the high-level bureaucracies she'd like to join. She really does have a doctorate, in Bilingual Ed, which means currently that she's employed to administer the high-school equivalency exams at the local community college. Last year she went to Central America for AID on a two-month contract but came back after only three weeks, full of anger and disgust at everyone from left to far right, except Archbishop Romero, and he is dead and canonized. A *de facto* canonization: Janice saw the votive offerings—letters, postcards, snapshots, statuettes, and flowers—the faithful left at his tomb. The tomb itself, she said, was a hastily laid slab of gray concrete, like the lid of the Hitler bunker.

Anyway Dr. B. put in a call to the embassy in Mexico City and asked the visa officer, when she finally got him on the line, if we couldn't have Roberto just long enough to let him speak at a meeting of the Bilingual Teachers Association. They meet each year in October, so it was no problem to schedule him, instead of Janice's presentation, which we've all heard a dozen times anyway.

"Is he really bilingual?" I asked.

"Julio says his French is excellent," Janice assured me.

We had been told a ten-day speaker's visa was the easiest to obtain. But by the time we phoned it was too late. Roberto had already applied for an ordinary tourist visa and had been told by the officer in charge, "There is no way we are going to let you into our country." Our invitation seemed like what it was, a feeble afterthought.

"Let's just go down to Juarez and pick him up and bring him across. Under the afghan in the back of my car. No one will bother to look. We'll just be a couple of crazy *gringas* on a shopping expedition," Janice phoned to say.

"We could buy a whole lot of paper flowers," I agreed, "or a really big *maceta*, the kind with glittering tiles stuck all over it." I thought of Ali Baba's thieves hiding in their jars. No I didn't, I thought of a customs official telling us to please step out of our vehicle while he went over it with a fine-tooth comb. Of course we didn't look like drug dealers, but at the border they have their orders. Jail would be a new experience, if it didn't last too long and if they put us all in the same cell, but the terror of those fifteen minutes I knew it would take them to search the car were too much for me, even in anticipation.

I said to Janice, "I don't see why Julio doesn't just go down to Mexico City, after all these years. If it was my brother, I'd run."

"Who knows what kind of papers Julio has. Maybe he's afraid if he leaves they won't let him back in."

Then I said, "You know, we really shouldn't be discussing this on the phone. I'll see you at work tomorrow. Or we could ask our senator for help. He might do something, on strictly humanitarian grounds."

"Twelve years in jail and it's not enough for them, those bastards," Janice fumed. Since she got back from Central America she's been a lot more outspoken and definite in her reactions to things. She used to worry about getting her name on the wrong mailing lists. Now she says she doesn't give a damn.

"Why do *you* have to go, why can't he just slip over after dark the way thousands do?" my husband wanted to know.

"He's been through too much already," I said. "If they picked him up, they'd deport him to Uruguay, but first he'd sit in jail again. It would be an awful mess."

"And if they pick you up?"

"They won't, they won't. All the times we've been to Juarez, when did they ever check us out? Who would look for contraband in Janice's old Volvo?" I had already imagined every possible sequence. They began by looking under the hood. They began by opening the trunk. They asked us to open our suitcases first. It always took them at least fifteen minutes to discover our clandestine passenger. What kind of face would I wear during those fifteen minutes?

"If his life were in danger, it would be another matter," my husband conceded. We were both thinking of his parents' escape from German-occupied Italy in forty-three, with the help of the Catholic underground. Such legends are dangerous things to outlive. My mother-in-law, by the time I met her, was the sort of woman who preached, "Your first duty is to your husband and children." Remembering her, I was driven to act.

"It's no big deal, really, we'll be back by Friday afternoon," I told my husband on Wednesday. Thursday we'd drive to the border, cross in, a piece of cake, meet Roberto, do our shopping, have dinner. We wouldn't check in at the same hotels, just in case. Early Friday we'd pick him up and he'd make himself comfortable in the back seat. I had already bought some fresh Dramamine in case he was the nervous type, like me. Somehow it worked out in my mind that if they discovered him sleeping it wouldn't be as bad for us as if they discovered him awake, alert, actively lying low. I replayed the actual moment of discovery a hundred times, trying to separate the border official, a woman perhaps—they could be the worst because of having to prove themselves—from other authority figures familiar from nightmares and interviews for jobs I didn't get. Cowardice is only poor thinking, a lack of clarity in one's ideas, I had been telling myself. Who are you afraid of anyway? It got to the point where I was reminding myself that the INS pull their pants on one leg at a time, like everyone else. I couldn't bring myself to imagine, as some books on mastering your fears suggest, a border guard stark naked, reduced to birthday suit vulnerability. What did all the other illegals do, I wondered, with their fear of getting caught? Maybe it was like getting mugged: after the first time you were more relaxed about it.

Nothing went quite as I'd imagined. Roberto was not frail like his brother in Albuquerque, and unlike other victims of the seventies' juntas I'd met he had no broken or cheap false teeth in the front of his mouth. He was big and robust-looking and genial and I could see Janice had a crush on him right away. She did not go into bilingual studies blindly.

When we went to buy the paper flowers, our decoy purchase, he insisted on choosing them himself, although Janice was paying.

"It's my funeral," he said. He couldn't speak a word of English. What he said was, *"Como es a mí a quien van a enterrar,"* and he chose the most garish pink roses they had in the store. Not because they appealed to him, but because they didn't. The main thing was, we let him decide. Next day he'd be our cargo. With the peso at a thousand to the dollar it made a lot of flowers. Janice said she'd give them to her Salvadoran maid when we got back.

"Listen to me, my maid, I sound like my middle-class friends in Mexico City. You've met Ceci, she cleans for me twice a week, has for the past five years, and I don't even know what kind of papers she has. What a life."

Janice and I drank a lot of wine and giggled all through dinner while Roberto smoked more than he ate and taught us prison slang from Libertad. Spanish is such a rich language by now. I could see he was sparing us the worst, however, which may have been delicacy but seemed to me like condescension toward two middle-aged ladies. Julio had told us his brother was twenty-three when they put him away, plus twelve and one year under civilian rule left him barely old enough to be our kid brother. I almost felt he was playing a part and I found it surprising in someone life has dealt such an inescapable assignment. With so much reality under his belt, why would he need to act? But not only was he playing a part in a little north-south comedy, he had assigned us roles as well and we had to accept them, whether they suited us or not. By the end of dinner he had blown so much smoke on our faces I had to remind myself, after all he's been through, whatever means of survival he's invented, he's entitled.

After dinner we went for a ride down the highway south of Juarez, toward Casas Grandes, the ruins I always wanted to visit but never had in my haste to reach the heart of the country. Janice had bought a lot of *ranchera* tapes and we played them loud with all the windows down. Roberto was driving and you could see the sincerity of that; after ten years indoors it meant a lot to him, even in someone else's car. Janice sat up front with him and I lay down in the back seat and pretended I was being smuggled across a border. Janice had forgotten her old afghan, the one the dog lies on when she takes him to the vet, which is fairly often, as he's been moribund for several years. She had faith in the efficacy of that doggy blanket. To replace it she bought one of those heavy plaids poor Mexicans use as mattresses. It was stiff and warm and we were headed toward safety. I fell asleep under the new blanket.

When I woke we were back in town in front of our hotel and Janice was dropping me off. "You wanted to phone home, right? Well it's already past ten. You know our husbands go to bed early." Then she and Roberto disappeared in a cloud of leaded smoke and I sat up till two, reading *Excelsior* and *Proceso* and *Uno más Uno,* which makes a pair of them, I thought to myself. By midnight I was so angry I almost phoned for a cab to take me to the bus station. It would have served them both right. *Uno más son dos. La pura evidencia.* It seemed like a dirty joke.

"One thing they don't tell you in the Amnesty International report is that prisoners get horny," Janice came in after two and fell onto her bed.

"Where were you?" I asked that foolish question.

"We went to a nightclub to hear some music and then for a ride along the river. It's terrible, they've got it all lit up at night like outside the state pen. No one can shack up in their cars any more, it would be indecent under those lights."

Janice's slang dated her but she didn't mind that it did, which in turn made her seem young again.

"I thought you wanted to cross back at break of day," I pouted.

"No problem," she said. "I set the alarm. What do you think of him?"

"I'll like him better in El Paso than I do in Juarez. I'm nervous about tomorrow."

"So is he. That's why I kept him up late. He really isn't in very good shape, did you notice? I don't know why we thought this was the better arrangement. He might just as well have stayed with us. I'll bet he hates to be alone in a room. That's what happens to people who have spent time in solitary. *El calabozo.*" She remembered the vocabulary lesson Roberto had given us at dinner.

"I thought we wanted to avoid creating a paper trail," I said. Janice didn't hear me. She was thinking hard. "Logistics," she sighed. Then she sprang up, called over her shoulder "I'll be right back," and was gone again. Fifteen minutes later, it was nearly three by now, she was back, with Roberto. She had him draped in the new blanket like a movie Mexican, his face completely covered.

"A dry run for tomorrow," she quipped. "We snuck up the back stairs. The *velador* was on the phone with his *novia.* He probably doesn't care anyway. I'll give him a big tip tomorrow morning. My God, do you realize, at a thousand pesos to the dollar, even I can be a big tipper."

I had stood up when Roberto came in.

"Oh please, don't let me disturb," he said, waiting for me to sit again before he allowed himself to collapse on the other bed. His shoes dropped to the floor, the blanket went back up over his head, and he lay motionless. Janice turned out the light and I made room for her next to me. I wondered if Roberto had been asleep when she'd knocked at the door of his room a few minutes before, and if the knocking had startled him. We're his jailers for now, I thought, feeling *la doctora*'s sharp elbow in my back. Then we all slept, the three of us in one small locked room, just as I'd imagined it.

It was ten before we reached the bridge next morning. We had planned to cross at eight with the morning flood but we overslept. Janice wasn't sure she had set the alarm properly. Maybe it rang and we didn't hear it. Or maybe it never rang at all. We were at the last traffic light before the bridge when she shouted, "Oh my God, I forgot the tequila!"

Ignoring my pleas, she swung around, a U-turn in the midst of oncoming traffic, cars honking on all sides. What faith she had in the drivers' reflexes.

"You know I always bring Jim a bottle of tequila. He'll be hurt if I forget. Besides, it's part of the plan, we have to have something to declare if they ask us. It gives them something to do, a one-step operation."

Roberto of course was under the blanket again by now. When we made that sudden turn, he must have wondered what was going on. While Janice was buying her liquor I leaned over the back seat to tell him. His shape under the blanket was huge and anthropomorphic. No one who looked closely could have imagined he was anything but a man, unless it was a corpse. The paper flowers we'd arranged on top of him had fallen to the floor. I didn't dare to pick them up.

"Roberto," I said softly, "Can you hear me?" He didn't move. I poked the blanket gently with one finger. Still no response. God, he must be frightened to death under there. How could we do this to him? (Easy, I could imagine Janice saying, we have U.S. passports and he doesn't.)

"We made a false start, Roberto, we had to stop and turn back again. From now on it's going to be easy," I spoke to the veiled inert form. It was like talking to someone who's not really there, a prisoner who isn't allowed to receive visitors. "So just hold tight, you hear?" I finished my speech. I could judge his fear by my own. He must have made a resolution not to move and was sticking to it with the tenacity that had kept him from going crazy during twelve years in Libertad, the very name of the place designed to drive you out of your mind.

I got through the next twenty minutes by reading the AAA guidebook I found in Janice's glove compartment. I started with Acambaro and was only up to Cuetzalan when they waved us on through. Without raising my eyes from the text I heard Janice compliment the customs lady on her complexion and extol the advantages of outdoor work.

We didn't pull over till just outside Roswell. We had to shake Roberto hard to wake him, both of us working on him at once. He got out and vomited by the side of the road. When I gave him the Dramamine, I never thought he'd take six at a time.

Janice was cross at first. "My God, do you realize," she scolded, "if they'd found you in that state, they could have accused us of abducting you." She tried to sound angry but I could see the idea appealed to her schoolmarm instinct for power over the lives of young men.

Roberto looked at us sadly and apologized for having left us to cope without him.

"What help could you have possibly been?" Janice wanted to know.

"I reasoned like an ostrich. If I can't see them, they can't see me. I made myself disappear."

"Roberto!" Janice was truly shocked. "That's the last thing we want you to do. Don't use that word." It took her half a minute to get started again. "Hey, now you're here in the land of the free, don't you want to kiss the ground, like the Pope? Here, I'll even make it more kissable for you." She unfurled a pink scented Kleenex at his feet.

Roberto had recovered by now. "I don't want to kiss your filthy ground," he drawled. And, fresh from being sick, he took our hands, mine first and then Janice's, and kissed them with such aplomb, I could see he had a great future in his new country.